"I do not want to st[ay]

Got it?"

Nolan swore mildly under his breath. "Don't think I won't throw you over my shoulder and carry you out of this courthouse if I have to, Mikki," he warned, his voice too intoxicating for a Nolan junkie like her to withstand.

"Try it," she dared him.

Unaffected by her empty threat, Nolan chuckled, then hauled her into the stairwell and pushed her up against the stone-cold wall after the metal door closed. His mouth clamped firmly over hers in a hot, openmouthed kiss that had her body humming.

She responded with equal hunger, ramming her fingers into his hair to make certain he knew without a doubt she'd settle for nothing less than complete satisfaction.

His knee nudged hers, and she shifted her stance to straddle his thigh. The snug fit of her skirt prevented her from feeling the pressure of his leg against her throbbing and swollen center. She moaned in frustration and hiked her skirt up past her hips.

Mikki's senses spun. Her body heated as if he'd set it on fire.

Thank heavens some things never changed.

Blaze™

Dear Reader,

As women we share a special kind of bond with other women, whether they are lifelong friends, special co-workers, family members, or sometimes even total strangers for a brief moment in time. But nothing is quite as special as that close bond between sisters, even sisters of the heart, such as the one Mikki Correlli shares with Lauren Massey (*On the Loose*, February 2005, by Shannon Hollis) and Rory Constable (*Slow Ride*, March 2005, by Carrie Alexander) in the LOCK & KEY trilogy.

Mikki knows she can count on her "sisters" to always be there for her, whether it's to tell her the truth when she needs to hear it or to offer their unwavering support when she really needs it. And boy, does she ever need them when her "ex-husband," Nolan Baylor, shows up with news she never expected to hear—that their divorce isn't valid!

Hard To Handle is a different kind of story for me, one I especially enjoyed not only because of the opportunity of working with Carrie and Shannon, but simply because of the journey it took me through.

I hope you enjoy Mikki and Nolan's journey to find their own happiness. I'd love to hear from you and know what you think! Please write to me at P.O. Box 39, Rouseville, PA 16344 or via e-mail at jamie@jamiedenton.net.

Until next time,

Jamie Denton

Books by Jamie Denton
HARLEQUIN BLAZE
10—SLEEPING WITH THE ENEMY
41—SEDUCED BY THE ENEMY
114—STROKE OF MIDNIGHT
    "Impulsive"
141—ABSOLUTE PLEASURE

Hard To Handle

JAMIE
DENTON

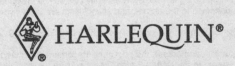

HARLEQUIN®

TORONTO • NEW YORK • LONDON
AMSTERDAM • PARIS • SYDNEY • HAMBURG
STOCKHOLM • ATHENS • TOKYO • MILAN • MADRID
PRAGUE • WARSAW • BUDAPEST • AUCKLAND

For my sisters,
Wanda, Stef, Frannie
and Lois
I love you all!

ISBN 0-373-79170-4

HARD TO HANDLE

1

"IS CHOCOLATE REALLY better than sex?" Michaela Correlli asked her sisters, licking a dollop of creamy dark chocolate from the tip of her index finger. Savoring the rich taste, she moaned with sheer hedonistic delight. "This stuff definitely qualifies as a front runner."

"Depends on the chocolate—and the man." Lauren Massey polished off her éclair and already had her eye on a second. "Not that I've had much by way of comparison lately," she added.

Mikki envied her younger sister's ability to eat whatever she wanted and not gain an ounce. If Mikki so much as considered indulging in a second of her older sister Aurora "Rory" Constable's scrumptious bakery goodies, she'd be relegated to the treadmill for the remainder of her natural life.

"These are a lot more satisfying than the last loser I laid." Mikki slid the delicate rose-patterned china plate in front of Lauren. "Maybe I should give up sex and stick to chocolate."

Rory held an oversize Lavender Field promotional

mug in her hand. "That'll be the day," she said, her green eyes warm with affection.

"I could, you know," Mikki said, a tad too defensively to be totally convincing.

Lauren snickered.

Mikki smoothed her hands down her slim black skirt as she rose to pour herself another cup of coffee from the big stainless-steel coffee urn in the corner of the back room of Rory's flagship bakery, Lavender Field. She shot them both a warning glance, which they ignored.

Lauren only laughed louder. "Not in this lifetime, Mikki Mantis."

Mikki gave the hem of her wine-colored blazer a sharp, indignant tug cringing at the nickname. They knew her too well. She had about as much hope of giving up sex as the San Francisco 49ers did of making it to another Super Bowl without the quarterbacking talents of Joe Montana or Steve Young. Some things in life just weren't meant to be. As long as Lauren or Rory didn't expect her to start mooning over some guy, then she figured no harm, no fumble.

"Are you going to tell us what was so important that it couldn't wait until Saturday?" Lauren asked. "I have a meeting with my managing editor, aka the Queen of Pain, in an hour."

Mikki returned to her stool and set the matching china cup on the scarred surface of the old butcher-block worktable. The air was redolent with the aromas of freshly baked bread and the dried bunches of lavender strung from the overhead beams. Since Rory had first opened Lavender Field, which had grown into one of the Bay area's most popular bakeries with a fourth location under development, Mikki and Lauren had been meeting here most Saturday mornings. Their weekly bull sessions touched on men, sex, hopes, dreams, men, sex, work, life, men, sex, films, books. No taboo subject existed between them.

Since Lauren and Rory weren't her sisters by blood, but of the heart, their relationship was even more precious to Mikki. Rory's mother, Emma, had been Mikki's foster mother from the time Mikki had been placed in the Constable home when social services had stepped in to remove her from a bad situation.

Twenty years later she still cringed whenever she recalled what a horrid little witch she'd been those first few months. Mouthy. Sullen. Sneaky… She'd ducked out one night and got herself busted for lifting a bag of potato chips from the corner liquor store. Another night, she'd been picked up by the cops on a curfew violation. All in all, she'd just made a general nuisance of herself. After cutting so many classes she now considered it a miracle she'd even made it out of the seventh grade. She hadn't made Emma Constable's job easy, but then, Mikki hadn't been expecting to stick around for long. Why would she when, at twelve, she'd already been shuffled through a half-dozen foster homes in less than two years?

Initially she'd kept her distance. She hadn't seen the point in becoming attached to people when they'd eventually call her social worker and toss her out because she wasn't worth the effort. Although she had instantly recognized that Emma wasn't like the other foster moms she'd been subjected to, she hadn't been dumb enough to believe the woman's earth-mother mask had been for real. In her experience, once the social worker dumped her and took off, the wholesome, all-American family facade faded fast and Mikki would be faced with a not-so-pleasant reality that consisted of foster parents who cared more about the state's monthly stipend than the kids in their care.

But Emma had eventually proven different. Months later the mask remained firmly in place, which had only added to Mikki's confusion. On the surface Emma's devotion to each of the children in her care appeared sincere. She'd been kind, fiercely protective and gently handed out discipline when warranted, the latter of which Mikki had earned plenty of during those first few months. Regardless of whatever stupid stunt she'd pulled, though, Emma's affection had remained steadfast. With an abundance of unconditional love, an unending supply of patience and her own odd brand of homespun wisdom, Mikki had eventually figured out that Emma Constable was the genuine article.

A number of troubled young girls had benefited from being placed in Emma's care over the years, but for the most part, they hadn't been long-term cases like herself and Lauren, who'd arrived four years after Mikki. Lauren had been fifteen, scared, confused and orphaned, and one year behind Mikki in school. As a matter of emotional survival, Mikki had made a habit of keeping people at a distance, but she'd done the unthinkable the day a group of preppies had picked on Lauren and had become her champion. Mikki had gone ballistic and ended up with a two-day suspension for fighting. To this day, she wasn't about to stand down when someone messed with her family.

She remembered expecting Emma to ground her for a month after that trick, but while the peace-prone Emma hadn't condoned Mikki's behavior, she hadn't exactly condemned it, either. Instead she'd encouraged Mikki to nurture her protective instincts in a more positive way. With Emma's guidance and encouragement, she'd become an attorney. She truly loved her work as a child advocate with San Francisco County Legal Aid, representing kids with backgrounds similar to her own who desperately needed someone in their corner.

A smile touched Mikki's lips as she pulled a pair of tickets from her handbag. "Because Saturday would be too late," she said, handing one to each of them. "These are only good for Friday night."

Rory set her mug on the table and shot Mikki a wry glance. "What's this all about?"

"A charity event." She sounded much too chipper, instantly raising her sisters' warning flags. They really did know her far too well.

"'Unlock the possibilities,'" Lauren read, then regarded Mikki with the same wariness as Rory. "Mikki, you're up to something."

Mikki took no offense at the accusation in Lauren's

tone. "Before either of you even think of saying no, it really is for a good cause." Forget playing a trump card, she'd go straight for the emotional jugular. "Maureen Baxter is hosting the event to raise money for a transitional home for young girls in crisis situations. With the shortage of qualified foster care, Baxter House will be an alternative to county housing."

What were once commonly known as orphanages or county homes were supposed to be safe havens, but overcrowded conditions and understaffing had all too often led to less than desirable environments that made the juvenile facilities an unfavorable option for displaced children.

"You know what nightmares those places can be," Mikki added, shooting Lauren a meaningful glance. "Courtesy of all the budget cutbacks, the situation is only becoming worse." Mikki and Lauren had both briefly lived at McClanin Hall, a county facility with a bad reputation due to its rough, prisonlike atmosphere. Rory had heard their horror stories and Mikki felt confident that that alone would be more than enough to push her sisters into conceding.

They both looked resigned, which made Mikki smile. Maureen Baxter, who was a couple of years younger than Mikki, had been another of Emma's girls. She had come along during Mikki's last year of high school after her mother had been killed by her abusive husband. Mikki wasn't as close to Maureen as she was to Lauren or to Rory, but they still shared a few bonds. Their affection and respect for the woman who'd cared for them for one, their work with children being another. As an attorney and child advocate for legal aid, the bulk of Mikki's caseload came from the child welfare division, where Maureen was employed as a social worker.

"If anyone can make it happen," she continued, "it'll be Maureen. She's one of the most compassionate, driven women I know." Mikki supported the cause completely, and had been working closely with Maureen, wading through the sea of legal red tape involved in such a huge undertaking.

"She already has the licensing," she told them. "Between what little government funding she's finagled, and the generosity of several financial contributors, she's close to turning Baxter House into a reality. She's having it built on that piece of raw land she inherited from her mother's estate. This event is to raise money for the building fund."

Lauren flicked her fingernail over the glossy black ticket with bright neon-pink lettering. "Fifty dollars?" she exclaimed, upon closer inspection. "Per person?"

"It's on me," Mikki reassured her. Fifty bucks wouldn't make a dent in Rory's wallet, and would leave only a small one in her own, but Lauren was a struggling journalist who worked for little more than peanuts half the time.

"Exactly what kind of possibilities are we supposed to unlock for fifty bucks?"

Rory leaned forward on the table, giving the éclairs she'd foresworn a longing look before resolutely wrapping her hands around the mug. "That's what I'd like to know."

"Ever hear of speed dating?"

"Sure," Lauren said with a shrug. "You pay an entry fee and then spend ten minutes chatting with some guy. If you hit it off, great. If he's a dud, then in ten minutes you're free to move on to the next one."

"Count me out." Rory plunked down her mug and stood.

"But—"

"Speed rejection is more like it. Forget it, Mikki," Rory said in that stubborn way of hers that drove Mikki even crazier than when she called her Mikki Mantis. "I'll reimburse you for the ticket and I'll fork over a nice-size donation, but there's no way I'm going to subject myself to that kind of humiliation."

"Oh, come on, Rory," she argued. "It's not *technically* speed dating. Actually, it's more like a key party. Sort of."

Looking even more dubious, Rory smoothed her sweater over her generous hips. "A key party? Like in *The Ice Storm*? You've got to be kidding. I thought those died out way back in the seventies, along with Mom's love beads and hookah pipe."

"Key parties are trendy again." Mikki grinned. "I hear hookahs are, too."

"I'm not the trendy type."

"Oh, I dunno, Rory," Lauren chimed in hopefully. "It might be fun."

"It *will* be," Mikki rallied. "Fifty dollars buys a key

or lock ticket. The male guests are all given keys and the women an adorable pendant in the shape of a tiny white-gold suitcase. Which, by the way, we get to keep. How can you say no to free jewelry, all for circulating, flirting and having fun trying to find out who holds the key to your locket? The guy with the key that opens your suitcase is your *date* for whatever prize is drawn from the raffle ticket hidden inside. Everybody wins."

Non-key-holder tickets were also available, but Mikki kept that fact to herself. She knew which option Rory would choose and, in Mikki's opinion, there was more to life than bread rolls and solitary annual excursions to France. Her sister desperately needed a life— even if she refused to admit it.

Rory still didn't look too convinced. "I don't know…"

Mikki understood her sister's hesitation, although she didn't agree with it. Rory was a beautiful, striking woman, but after an awkward adolescence plagued by weight problems and few dates, coupled with a nasty breakup with her only long-term boyfriend, she was now painfully self-conscious about her figure. Having more than a few hang-ups of her own, Mikki couldn't completely discount Rory's apprehension.

"Oo-oh," Lauren murmured, putting down her ticket to pluck a flyer from Mikki's purse. "The grand prize is an all-inclusive weekend in Mendocino at the Painter's Cove Resort. The winners share a luxury suite with a hot tub and private pool." A lascivious grin canted her lips. "I could handle that."

"A weekend with a total stranger," Rory reminded them. "It could end up being the blind date from hell."

"Or not," Lauren said, opening the brochure. "Tennis, golf, horseback riding on the beach. Even an on-site spa. Oh, my God—they have mud baths and hot stone massages."

Rory shuddered. "A *naked* weekend with a total stranger."

"No one says you actually have to go on the date with the guy," Mikki pointed out. "Look, Maureen's been working hard on this event and is counting on *all* of us being there to support her. The backing from city merchants has been amazing."

Lauren perused the extensive list of prizes, then handed the brochure to Rory. "It looks like every movieplex in the entire Bay area has donated passes."

Rory brightened. "Movie passes? Now you're talking my language."

"Tons of them," Mikki said. "Including the theaters, the opera house—even the ballet company. They were all happy to hand over almost a dozen pairs of tickets. Maureen's gotten just about every trendy or exclusive restaurant in San Francisco to each contribute three or more dinners for two, and even managed to wrangle nearly a third of the B and B's in Napa to donate weekend stays. There are a couple of day-spa packages, too. I would love to get my hands on one of those."

"She really worked hard on this," Rory said. "It looks like every lock-and-key ticket holder will receive a prize of some sort."

Mikki sensed her weakening and went in for the proverbial kill. "Baxter House is important to her. And to me, too. I wish there'd been a place like that when I was in the system," she added, hoping it would be the final push over the edge into acceptance.

Rory let out a sigh, then placed the brochure on the table before crossing the workroom to pull a lavender apron from the hook by the rear door. "I'll reimburse you for my ticket, but I don't need to be there."

"Well…" Mikki hesitated. She wasn't all that comfortable the key party plan herself. When it came to men, she didn't exactly wear a user-friendly label. The truth was, she had a tendency to use men for sex. She had no use for relationships or romantic entanglements. The female version of the old love-'em-and-leave-'em cliché. "You sorta do."

Rory slipped the loop of the apron over her head and tied the sash. "Why, exactly, do I *sorta* have to be there?"

"Because I kind of promised Maureen you'd…" Oh, she'd really done it this time. Rory was going to kill her.

Her sister's eyes instantly filled with suspicion. "That I'd what, Mikki?"

"Donate desserts and pastries from the shop," she said in a rush.

Rory folded her arms, raised one eyebrow and gave her a direct look. "For how many people?" Her sister obviously knew a rat—even one with good intentions— when she smelled one.

Lauren nudged Mikki with her elbow. "Have you

ever noticed how much she looks like Mom when she does that? Scary."

"I always hated that look," Mikki muttered.

"Because you knew she'd busted you cold," Lauren reminded her.

"Well?" Rory impatiently prodded.

Mikki sucked in a quick breath that did nothing to alleviate the stab of guilt. "Five hundred." She winced before adding, "Minimum."

Lauren's eyes rounded in surprise. "Mikki, you've always been pushy, but even you have to admit this time you just may have crossed the line."

"I think I figured that one out, Lauren."

"Are you for real?" Rory's tone rose sharply, but contained no anger, only shocked disbelief.

Mikki couldn't really blame her if she was angry. She *had* resorted to out-and-out manipulation, even if it was for Rory's own good. Since she'd opened Lavender Field she'd been working too hard and it was time she let loose and had a little fun. Although whipping up baked goods for five-hundred-plus people didn't exactly qualify as fun, she suddenly realized.

"I'll help," Mikki offered. She was a much better lawyer than a cook, and hoped her sister would forget that minute detail.

"Prepare baked goods and pastries for five hundred people or more with only four days' notice?" Rory's expression remained tough as nails even though she had an expert staff at her disposal. "You bet you will."

"So will I," Lauren added, leaning over to offer Mikki a sympathetic hug.

Rory shook her head. "Dammit, Mikki. I can't believe you did this to me."

"I know, and I'm sorry. I should be shot. But think of all the great publicity for Lavender Field. With your fourth store opening soon, it can't hurt."

"Maureen's really expecting five hundred people to show up for this thing?" Lauren asked.

"She's hoping for twice that," Mikki answered. "She's sold five hundred tickets so far."

"Impressive, but that's hardly going to cover the cost of construction," Rory pointed out.

"Maureen found a contractor willing to donate the work for free, and is arranging for subcontractors who'll do the same. All she has to do is raise enough to cover the cost of materials," Mikki explained. She turned to Lauren. "Could you do a story on the fundraiser? This is San Francisco. You know how we love our causes. Who knows what kind of additional donations it might bring in for Baxter House. Maureen would love the free publicity."

"Maybe," Lauren said with a fair degree of hesitation, but Mikki could tell by her sister's expression she was giving serious consideration to the idea.

"Maybe you should ask Maureen first," Rory chided with a hint of sarcasm.

Mikki shot Rory an exasperated look. "I said I was sorry. Sheesh, do you want it in blood?"

Rory's wry smile was slow in coming. "Flour will

do just fine. And you'd better be here by six o'clock to start signing. Call it just deserts for volunteering my services." She snorted. "And risking my dignity at a key party, of all things."

Mikki she loved these women with all her heart. And it had nothing whatsoever to do with the fact they never could say no to her.

BALANCING THREE DRINK glasses in her hands, Mikki nodded her thanks to the bartender then navigated the crush of charity-loving partygoers at Clementine's to make her way back to the table where Rory and Lauren waited for her. A particularly attractive denim-covered ass caught her attention and she paused momentarily to check out the rest. Trim waist, wide shoulders and…oops. That little gold band on his left hand was more than enough of a deterrent for her to keep walking. Still, that ass definitely deserved a second glance and she shamelessly enjoyed the view as she passed.

A stocky guy with dark wavy hair sporting a small, twinkling diamond in his ear blatantly gave her the once-over as she moved closer to Rory and Lauren. Under normal circumstances, Mikki didn't go out of her way to encourage men who came on to her, but she'd had a brutally disappointing day in court. She still couldn't believe the judge had ordered the minor she'd been representing back into his junkie, trick-turning mother's custody when the child's paternal grandparents were willing to assume his care. Despite Mikki's strenuous objections, the judge had ruled in favor of the boy's biological mother, but Mikki knew from experience the kid would be back in the system within a few months, with who knew how many new emotional scars.

The guy with the earring winked at her. Maybe some safe but mindless sex would take the edge off, she thought. She usually preferred the role of the aggressor. Her party, her rules. As long as she called the shots, she stayed in control, which was the only way she liked it.

Diamond Jim did have a pair of gorgeous, clear green eyes that perhaps made him worthy of a pithy innuendo about locks and keys. At least until he nudged the guy next to him and made an obscene gesture about the generous size of her breasts.

She considered pouring her drink over his head as she passed, but couldn't justify wasting a perfectly good diet soda on a classless jerk. Instead, she shot him a cold look and kept moving.

In an era where reed-thin models graced the covers of nearly every magazine on the stands, she had the kind of body that had gone out of fashion five decades ago. As one of her previous lovers had told her after she'd shown him the exit, she had a body made for sin, but the heart of an ice queen.

She'd laughed in his face as she held the door open for him, all because he'd kept pressing her for a commitment. She'd warned him she wasn't into exclusive relationships, but he hadn't listened. Why was the concept of a no-strings affair so difficult to grasp? Men did it all the time, but when a woman wanted to do the same, she was called coldhearted or worse. She'd already found and lost her one true love—if such a thing even existed—but it had ended badly and she had no desire to repeat the experience. *Ever.*

"Don't you just love a good buffet?" Lauren said when Mikki reached their table, now laden with small oval platters, one of them heaped with various tidbits and a small sampling of the goodies from Rory's shop—thankfully prepared by Rory and her competent staff. Rory had lightened up and hadn't forced Mikki to actually keep her word when she'd arrived to help. She'd even added a prize of her own to the cause with a day behind the scenes at Lavender Field along with a month's supply of baked goods.

"Who wouldn't?" Mikki answered, carefully setting their drinks amid the array of food. "There's always bound to be just the right combination to sate most any appetite." She paused while handing Lauren her drink to blatantly follow the progress of a tall, athletically built Adonis with sun-kissed blond hair and a confident swagger striding toward the black-and-white-tiled dance floor.

Rory made a minor adjustment to the shimmering lilac shawl draped loosely over her shoulders before taking a tentative sip of her white wine. "I have a feeling she's not talking about the food," she said to Lauren over the din of conversation.

"Does she ever think of anything besides sex?" Lauren returned with a laugh, taking her drink from Mikki.

Mikki perched on the stool and carefully tugged down the hem of her short, black sleeveless dress. "Not really," she said, before taking a sip of soda. God, what she wouldn't give for a real drink. She'd even settle for one of Lauren's favored frou-frou blended numbers—a sign of true desperation.

Lauren let out a weighty sigh. "Don't you ever want more from a relationship than sex?"

"Sex *is* the only relationship I'm interested in, thank you very much." A long and lean stud looked her way. She smiled at him and slowly lifted the delicate white-gold chain around her neck, the small suitcase charm Maureen had given her upon arriving swinging enticingly in front of her cleavage. His deep-set eyes filled with regret as he shrugged and displayed empty hands.

She let out a sigh. Damn. No key. Not every guest at Clementine's had opted to purchase a lock or key ticket, although they had paid the rather steep entrance fee to the private party. The few moments she'd had to speak to Maureen upon arriving, her friend had been ecstatic about the money being raised for Baxter House. There'd even been a sizable donation from one of the wealthy and privileged Telegraph Hill set.

"Don't you ever look at a guy—like him for instance—" Lauren inclined her head in the keyless stud's direction "—and wonder if he could be the one?"

Mikki forced a laugh. She'd found "the one" once and, as a matter of self-preservation, she'd pushed him away. Hell would freeze over before she ever went there again. She had too many skeletons in her closet and preferred to keep them locked away, something a serious relationship wouldn't permit, not when trust required a certain level intimacy she had no interest in exploring.

Keep it simple, keep it short, keep them from getting close enough to see what she kept hidden in the closet. That was her motto, and she was sticking to it—with the tenacity of a pit bull.

"The one to make me scream with pleasure?" she replied with her usual flippancy whenever Lauren started with the Cinderella propaganda. "All the time."

"No," Lauren said, her tone serious. "Settle down. Buy real estate." She studied the creamy liquid in her glass, appropriately called a White Knight. "Have a family."

"I don't need a man for that," Mikki said with more brittle laughter. "Just a better-paying job." She let out a weary sigh. "I don't have the intrinsic need most women do to nest. I'm a realist, Lauren. Not a romantic."

Lauren lifted her clear hazel gaze to give her a pointed look. "What about a family?"

Mikki shrugged, but the unexpected weight settling on her shoulders refused to budge. "You, Rory and Mom are my family." She downed a large portion of her diet cola. The sorry substitute did nothing to quell the sudden sharp craving for something a whole lot more potent than an innocuous soft drink.

"I meant a family of your own," Lauren pressed. "You'd make a great mother, Mikki. I hope you realize that someday."

No way. Not her. *Never.*

She knew exactly what her sister meant and she resented the reminder. She suffered with more sorrow than she'd ever admit to over her decision to never have children. But she couldn't change the past. She was who she was—a Correlli. And the bloodline ended with her. Period. She'd learned to accept her fate—why wouldn't anyone else?

But something deep in Mikki's chest still caught and squeezed hard anyway. It *wasn't* the sharp pang of longing. Or was it? Maybe it was another one of those annoying ticks from her biological clock that hadn't caught on that Correllis had no business breeding. She kept hitting the snooze button, but every so often the what-ifs managed to sneak past her barriers to tweak her self-pity nerve. She couldn't change who or what she was: the last woman who should ever consider having a baby.

"Motherhood doesn't interest me," she said a tad too snappishly. Guilt instantly slammed into her at the flash of hurt in Lauren's eyes.

Shit. She hadn't meant to sound so cold, but Lauren was hitting a nerve she didn't appreciate having nudged. What was done was done. And she'd gotten over it a lifetime ago.

"You're wonderful with kids." Rory tugged her shawl tighter around her shoulders. "Don't sell yourself short."

"Just as long as they belong to someone else," she reminded Rory. "When you two decide to start having babies, count on me to spoil them rotten. Now, can we please change the subject before I break out in hives?"

A server neared and Mikki signaled to place another order. She would have sold her soul and then some for a something strong enough to anesthetize her mind. She loved Lauren but, dammit, she had no desire to navigate an emotional obstacle course.

The server took his sweet time coming their way, giving the craving gnawing at her time to build. Her hands trembled, so she fisted them in her lap and attempted to concentrate on the rich red-and-gold, bordelloesque decor of Clementine's. The need for a shot of bourbon only grew stronger. After four years of sobriety, it annoyed the life out of her that she still had to fight off such strong temptation for a drink—for several drinks—but she'd learned early on that some days were easier to get through than others.

She dug her nails into her palms as the server finally approached. "There's a twenty in it for you if you're back in less than five minutes," she told him, placing an order for another two glasses of soda and another round for Lauren and Rory.

Opening her black silk evening bag, she pulled out her car keys and set them in front of Rory for safekeeping. "Just in case," she said tightly. "It's one of those days."

Rory's expression instantly filled with concern, but Mikki shook her head, signaling she didn't want to discuss the war going on inside her. She'd get through this, just as she always did. One second at a time if necessary. Ridding herself of her car keys was merely a precaution.

Contrition clouded Lauren's eyes. Reaching across the table, she gave Mikki's hand a light squeeze. "I shouldn't have said anything. I'm sorry."

She looked at Lauren and tried to offer her a reassuring smile, but could only manage a slight grimace. "Forget about it," she said with as much sincerity as she could muster. "I already have."

A lie. A big fat one, but she wasn't about to hurt Lauren's feelings further or cause either of her sisters more worry. Mikki's ghosts were her problem.

She knew they were only concerned about her, and with good reason, but she wasn't about to blow all her hard work because of a silly reminder that she'd willingly chucked her own glass slipper out the window. She'd made her choices and, for the most part, was perfectly content with her life. She had a job she loved, a small but close circle of friends and her odd, mismatched family. If she needed a man, she found one to ease her frustration. On those occasions between lovers, she took care of her needs the way any woman with a healthy sex drive did—by making sure there were plenty of batteries on hand.

The server returned in record time. As Mikki paid him and included the bonus she'd promised, Rory said something she didn't quite catch, but the urgency in her voice had Mikki looking up to follow her sister's gaze.

There wasn't enough alcohol in Clementine's to numb her. Not when she found herself gazing at a pair of familiar dark brown bedroom eyes she'd never been able to forget, no matter how many vices she abused to banish them from her mind.

The buzz of conversation, the raucous beat of the music and the colorful changing lights from the dance floor faded. Rory's hand settled on her arm, but Mikki took no comfort from the supportive gesture as she returned the stare of the one man she'd hoped to never see again—Nolan Baylor.

Her heart gave a sudden traitorous lurch. *Damn.*

The passage of time had been good to him. His shoulders seemed wider than she remembered and his biceps, emphasized by the snug fit of the sleeves of the dark, charcoal-gray polo shirt he wore, were definitely thicker. His waist appeared leaner, too, but he still possessed the same rugged good looks she'd always preferred.

A slow, sinful smile tipped his mouth. The lines of his face were more angular now, too, she realized. Sharper. Harder. Just like the challenging glint in his eyes.

Every step that brought him closer filled her with tension.

His smile deepened.

A flash of silver caught the light. Apprehension slid down her spine, chilling her. Dangling from her ex-husband's long, tanned fingers was a small white-gold key.

2

MIKKI WAS EVEN MORE beautiful than Nolan remembered. Seeing her again had him recalling plenty, too. Not just how incredibly sexy she looked in that skimpy black dress clinging to her voluptuous curves, but the passion and how they'd never been able to get enough of each other. The laughter, the good times and, unfortunately, the arguments and mistakes made by two people who'd been too young and headstrong were equally prominent.

Mikki always did have a short fuse. One look reminded him of just how volatile she could be as her shock segued into apprehension, followed by a distinct flare of hot temper evident in those sapphire-blue eyes that defied her heritage.

"What the hell are you doing here?"

Not the greeting he'd hoped for, yet no less than he'd expected, or even deserved, for that matter. "Nice to see you again, too, Mikki," he said, tucking the key into his pocket.

"The name is Michaela," she said with an unmistakable chill. "Only people I care about call me Mikki."

A smarter man than he would've taken her icy retort as a signal to keep his distance. God knew they could be poison to each other, but that hadn't ever kept them apart for long in the past. Probably because the makeup sex had always been phenomenal. Besides, when it came to the onyx-haired, curvaceous spitfire with contempt in her eyes as she stared at him, he never had been all that bright.

"Is that any way to greet an old…" He intentionally left her hanging. Behind him, his oldest friend, Tucker Schulz, muttered something about a death wish. "…Friend?"

Mikki shifted nervously on her stool, then issued a short, derisive bark of laughter. Her hand trembled as she reached blindly for her drink. The contents sloshed close to the rim and she shot him another frosty glare. "That isn't the term I'd use."

He chuckled. "No, I don't imagine you would." Any one of the choice phrases she'd occasionally hurled at him whenever he'd riled her hot Sicilian and fiery Irish blood were no doubt already hovering on her tongue.

Before the night ended, he thought, she'd have more than enough opportunity.

After the way they'd parted, with her calling him a selfish, egotistical bastard and him responding with equally hateful words he wasn't exactly proud of, he hadn't expected her to welcome him back to San Francisco with open arms. If she was this ticked off at just seeing him, she'd rupture something vital when she learned he'd moved back for good. And that was only the beginning.

He'd anticipated her anger, but he sure as hell hadn't been prepared for the stirring of his blood. An unfortunate miscalculation on his part, he decided, because he really should have been prepared for nothing less. He might be older, but he'd just been handed proof he hadn't gained an ounce of wisdom where Mikki was concerned.

The passion between them had always been white-hot and explosive, but in the end, it hadn't been enough to keep them together. He understood now their relationship had been built on sexual attraction, which hadn't prepared either of them for the day-to-day struggles of marriage, let alone coping with the problems that eventually led to their divorce.

"You remember Tuck," he said, needing a diversion. He stepped aside in hopes of allowing his libido a chance to cool. Not that he actually believed it possible now that he was within touching distance of her again. She was the kind of woman that dug under a man's skin. And stayed there.

"Oh, my God. Tuck." A genuine smile softened her expression as she came off the bar stool and moved right past him to greet Tucker with a warm hug. "It's been such a long time," she said, stepping back. "You're looking yummy. What have you been doing with yourself?"

"As little as possible." Tucker gave her an appreciative once-over. "Since you and Nolan split, he's taken to working hard enough for both of us."

She made no comment, not that Nolan expected her

to. Slipping her arm through Tuck's, she steered him toward the table. "I don't think you've ever met my sisters. Rory Constable," she said, indicating a woman Nolan hardly recognized. Mikki's older sister had matured into an elegant, Rubenesque beauty. The Rory he remembered had been a friendly frump in granny glasses and long hair, a golden retriever following on the heels of her Birkenstock sandals.

"And this is Lauren Massey." She looked to her sisters. "Tucker Schulz. He and Nolan have been friends for..." She smiled at Tucker, studiously ignoring Nolan.

"More years than I care to keep track of," Tucker returned with a dimple-deepening grin as he eyed Lauren. His gaze then skimmed over Rory. She stared into a glass of white wine, her complexion becoming ruddy.

Mikki cast a quick, nervous glance in Nolan's direction before turning back to Tucker. "I'd offer to buy you a drink, but I was just leaving." Rising up onto her toes, she reached across the table for a set of keys in front of Rory. The hem of her slinky black dress hiked up a good two inches to reveal her shapely thighs. More than his blood stirred as Nolan took in his fill.

Rory lifted her gaze in time to beat her to the keys. She slid them off the table and into her handbag. "Actually," she said with a hint of a smile on her lips, "we've only just arrived."

He didn't miss the heated glare Mikki shot her sister or how Rory's smile shifted into a distinct retaliatory smirk.

Lauren suddenly looked very uncomfortable. "If

you'll excuse me," she said quietly, slipping off the red-padded stool. "I'll catch up with you later."

He knew how Mikki's mind worked. No doubt she considered Lauren's abrupt desertion and Rory's non-compliance as a betrayal, but one she'd easily forgive. When Mikki loved, she did so with her entire heart, no holds barred. He'd seen it in the way she'd always looked out for her sisters and in the little things she'd once done for him. Like the times she'd wait up for him to come home from whatever crappy job he'd been working to help support them, even though she'd had an early class in the morning. Or the time she'd skipped classes for a week and refused to leave the apartment because he'd been knocked on his rear end by a nasty flu bug.

Tucker took the stool Lauren vacated and caught the attention of a passing waiter.

Mikki snatched her purse from the table. "I have a sudden need for fresh air."

"Good idea." Nolan came up behind her, fighting the need to touch her, to skim his hands over the generous dips and swells of her bombshell curves. He fished the white gold key out of his pocket. "I'll join you."

She stiffened. "That won't be necessary," she said tightly.

He dipped his head to whisper in her ear. "Now what kind of gentleman would I be if I let you wander out-side all on your own at night?"

The scent of her cologne teased him, resurrecting an-other long-forgotten memory. They'd been in law school, a time when he'd rarely had more than a couple of quarters to rub together. He'd taken on a tutoring job to earn extra money to buy her a stupid bottle of expensive perfume for Christmas. He'd be a fool to read too much into the fact that she still wore the scent, but that didn't prevent the razor-thin slice of satisfaction from knifing through his common sense.

"'Gentleman'?" She pulled away and pinned him with her gaze. "I wouldn't use that term where you're concerned, either."

Selfish prick, more likely.

"Ouch," he said, gripping his chest in a mocking gesture.

Facing Tucker, Mikki said, "Good to see you again, Tuck." She cast a look in Rory's direction and mouthed something he couldn't see but that sent Tuck's eyebrows skyward.

Swiping one of the tall, narrow glasses from the table in front of her, she quickly drained the contents, then exchanged the empty for the full one to carry with her. She bolted toward the back of the bar to the outdoor deck with its inspiring view of the harbor. He admired the brisk swing of the black fabric covering her sweet, rounded ass. How could one woman have that much power? he wondered, feeling as if he were tied in knots he'd never unravel.

He let out a sigh and turned to Rory. "I get the feeling she's not too happy to see me." He'd always liked Rory, but he wasn't about to hazard a guess as to whether she currently returned the sentiment. Rory's devotion to her sisters was as fierce as Mikki's protectiveness of them.

"Can't say I blame her," she said without an ounce of sympathy.

Neither could he, but after all this time he'd thought Mikki's temper might have cooled. At least a little. Apparently all that hot blood in her veins ran deeper than he'd anticipated. He only hoped she hadn't inherited her ancestral desire for vendettas or he'd be a dead man before midnight.

Tucker clapped a hand on his shoulder. "Good luck, pal."

"Thanks, I'm gonna need it."

"You'll need more than that when she finds out you're back in town for good," Tucker reminded him. "And why you're here tonight."

Tuck had a point. "Know where I can get a deal on a bulletproof vest?"

Now that he thought about it, full body armor sounded like a wise choice. And some riot gear. A few stiff shots of tequila to bolster his courage couldn't hurt, either.

He left his friend in Rory's capable hands and took off for the bar, placing an order for a Mexican boilermaker, a double shot of Cuervo Gold with a beer chaser. As he waited for the bartender to return, a leggy redhead sidled up beside him with a smile that promised ample warmth against the evening chill. Once upon a time he would've taken advantage of the blatant come-on, but after Mikki, he just hadn't been all that interested in other women. Besides, he hadn't shelled out a sizable donation to Maureen Baxter's pet cause to ensure he'd be given the key to Mikki's locket because he'd been in a generous mood. He and Mikki had unfinished business.

"You look like you'd be a perfect fit," the redhead purred, showing off the locket wedged between her impressive cleavage.

He wasn't so much as tempted. "Sorry. This key is spoken for."

She let out a breathy sigh. "Pity."

He shrugged apologetically, unmoved by her practiced pout or her sleek curves wrapped in glittering electric blue. The redhead sashayed away, her attention already on another prospective key holder.

Drumming his fingers impatiently on the highly polished wood of the bar, he debated the wisdom of showing up at Clementine's. He'd always been more of an adventurer than a deep thinker, preferring instead to move on with the business of living. There were easier avenues he could've taken, and he almost wished he'd given his half-witted plan to catch Mikki off guard more thought. Unfortunately the pressure from the senior partners to tie up a financially hazardous loose end quickly before finalizing the partnership agreement hadn't left him much time to carefully consider his options. And he did have a responsibility to the firm he couldn't ignore.

Initially he hadn't paid much attention to the buzz around the office about the key party until he'd happened to overhear a trio of paralegals mention that Maureen Baxter was the driving force behind the fundraiser. He'd been fairly certain Mikki would somehow be involved in the cause, so he'd placed a call to Maureen. Not only had she confirmed his suspicions, but he'd impulsively purchased two key-holder tickets along with the promise of a very sizable donation if Maureen guaranteed him the key to Mikki's locket.

At first Maureen had staunchly refused—and he did appreciate her alliance to Mikki—but when he'd upped the ante, her ethics had taken a back seat to the money he'd promised to add to the coffer. To insure she wouldn't suffer second thoughts, he'd doubled his original offer and had his assistant show up at Maureen's office with a check in exchange for the key he wanted. In return, he'd received a pair of keys, one clearly marked for his use; the other he'd planned to give to Tucker.

Fingering the trinket in his palm, he didn't harbor an ounce of guilt for buying Maureen's cooperation. He did, however, carry more than a doubt or two about why he'd gone to such extreme. Granted, the news he had to deliver would best be served in person, but it sure didn't necessitate a donation large enough to cover a respectable percentage of the funds needed for the building of Baxter House. Mikki would be livid when she found out what he'd done and, worse, why he'd done it.

Convincing Tucker to come with him hadn't been an easy feat, but when Tuck's sisters and sisters-in-law had ganged up on him, his long-time friend hadn't stood a chance. The irony of the situation hadn't been lost on him. As Tuck had gleefully pointed out, the first time Nolan had ever used the money and influence he'd run from most of life, it was to guarantee him a night with a woman who'd rather eat ground glass than be with him.

The bartender finally showed up with the tequila and beer, and Nolan immediately threw back the Cuervo, followed by a hefty swallow of the ice-cold Dos Equis that failed to alleviate the burning in his gut. Whether the booze or his unexpected physical reaction to Mikki was the cause, he couldn't be sure. Quite frankly, he doubted it made a difference. In the end, he'd probably never understand the emotional hold she had on him.

He polished off his beer and debated ordering another. Five years ago when he'd left the Bay area, he hadn't expected to ever return, at least not for good. After making a name for himself in Los Angeles, he'd been offered the position of managing partner at Turner, Crawford and Lowe with the caveat that he head up the family law division in the firm's San Francisco offices. As much as it grated his nerves, he understood he'd initially been hired by the prestigious firm because of the Baylor name, but he'd earned the partnership by working his ass off and consistently racking up more billable hours than any other associate in the firm.

Once the buy-in was complete, he'd be one of three managing partners running the Bay area office of the

Southern California-based firm. He already held the responsibility of monitoring the caseload of close to two dozen associates, a quad of law clerks anxiously awaiting bar exam results and twice as many paralegals plus numerous support personnel. In addition, he still managed his own caseload, which ran the gamut from more high-profile divorce actions to adoptions, all the way down to custody matters, as well as support and visitation modifications. He loved it all, too, which was a helluva difference from the live-hard-play-harder-but-leave-a-good-looking-corpse philosophy he'd cultivated most of his life.

He left the bar and made his way to the deck in search of Mikki. He supposed in part he had her to thank for his success. When they'd separated, he'd honored the Baylor family tradition by turning into a classic workaholic. He'd buried himself in his work, using the law as a means of survival because it'd been preferable to facing the truth—that by walking away from his marriage, he really was no better than the bastard of a father he despised.

Another of his less than sterling moments.

The truth was even tougher to face: that he hadn't had the balls to tell Mikki he'd never wanted the divorce in the first place. As much as he tried to convince himself he'd been young and filled with an overdose of foolish pride, a semblance of wisdom did blossom with age. If faced with the same set of circumstances, he liked to believe this time around he wouldn't hesitate to make the right choice, rather than behave like a selfish prick all because she'd filleted his ego by adamantly refusing to have a baby.

Based on her reaction tonight, convincing Mikki he'd changed wouldn't be easy. Not that it mattered what she thought of him. They were finished a long time ago. Or were they?

He paused near the open, glass double doors. Did it make a difference what she thought of him? Had he merely acted in his usual impulsive manner or was there another motive he hadn't been aware existed for ensuring Mikki would be his date for whatever prize her locket held?

The answer had him taking in a deep, unsteady breath. He couldn't possibly be thinking in terms of second chances.

Could he?

He hadn't wanted the divorce, even if he had run at the first sign of trouble in their marriage. He blamed immaturity and pride. She no doubt blamed him—period.

Still, he thought with a twitch of his lips, in their time apart he had learned to appreciate the value of patience and determination. An asset he figured he'd be calling on in abundance tonight, because once he informed her their divorce had all the validity of a fake ID, she'd no doubt push him to the limit.

Provided she didn't shoot him on the spot.

WHAT THE HELL was Nolan doing here?

Mikki rested her arms on the smooth redwood railing and clutched her glass of cola firmly in her hand.

The need to indulge in something stronger hadn't waned so much as a fraction.

Just one drink, she thought. One. That's all she needed.

Except she knew better. One was never enough. That first bitter taste of bourbon hitting her tongue would only be the beginning. The soothing warmth sliding down her throat was as much of an addiction as was the welcoming buzz of alcohol hitting her bloodstream. She'd have another, and another, until she'd numbed herself into a drunken stupor.

She leaned forward and lifted her face to gaze at the stars blanketing the darkened sky over the Pacific, then took in a long, unsteady breath. Partially hidden behind the cover of a bushy potted juniper, she tried ignored the few couples braving the damp night air to cuddle together away from the crush of the crowd inside Clementine's. A piercing stab of envy reduced her diligence to not think about how alone she felt in comparison to mere wishful thinking.

A tremor passed over her skin, but she didn't hold the cold Pacific breeze culpable, or her own foolishness in venturing outdoors without the benefit of a sweater to ward off the brisk chill of the May evening. Oh, no. Nolan held that honor. His unexpected presence was responsible for the shock waves of too many emotions to articulate rolling through her.

If she wasn't careful, she'd roll right up to the bar and order a shot of bourbon to add to her cola.

What possible motive could he have for being in San Francisco?

She struggled to keep her teeth from chattering as she moved deeper into the shadows. His return could have something to do with the probate of his father's estate, except Nolan had never made any secret of the fact that he rejected everything his rich, influential father represented. When she'd gone to pay her final respects to her former father-in-law, whom she'd only met on two occasions, it hadn't exactly escaped her notice that the powerful state legislator's son had been notably absent.

And to think Nolan had once possessed the gall to call her coldhearted because she didn't want children. The man could write a bestseller on cool detachment. She'd even gone to her own father's funeral—and she'd hated everything about the man who'd molested his own daughter.

Out of habit, she immediately shoved that unpleasant thought back into the closet where it belonged. Opening the clasp on her evening bag, she searched for the pack of emergency cigarettes she always carried with her. She and Nolan hadn't always been at each other's throats or circled like wary hounds afraid to say the wrong thing. There'd been a time when they hadn't been able to get enough of each other. She missed those lazy Sunday mornings they'd spent in bed, making love most of the day and only surfacing long enough to regain their strength. She missed how they used to debate case law or talk about the future—before he'd ruin it by bringing up the subject of family. At first she'd change the subject or remain noncommittal, but after a while he'd to become more insistent until she'd finally told him the truth—she wouldn't ever have a child with him. She hadn't offered an explanation beyond she wasn't the mothering type.

She hadn't always felt that way about children, and whether or not her fears were unreasonable, in her opinion, she had no business having babies when she was having trouble controlling her addiction to alcohol. Besides, she already had two strikes against her: an abusive father and a mother who'd abandoned her. Everyone knew three strikes and you were out.

Suddenly she felt much older than her thirty-two years. She slipped a long slim from the pack, then dug out the disposable lighter and lit up. She inhaled deeply, taking the smoke into her lungs, waiting for the familiar calm to wash over her to curb the need for a drink. But the substitute failed to provide on all counts. No vice in existence was capable of calming her rattled composure tonight.

Studying the reflection of the twinkling lights on the surface of the water below, she smoked her cigarette and listened to the sound of the rising tide. Not even the gentle lap of water against the thick pylons could sooth her.

When she thought of everything she'd thrown away to protect her secrets…the lies she'd told to the one person she should've trusted the most…

She let out a regret-filled sigh. She'd been twenty-three and at the start of her second year as law student at Berkeley when she'd met Nolan. With no interest in another messy romantic entanglement after her last disastrous relationship, she'd initially tried to ignore him. Except her dismissal had made him even more relentless. Only a woman without a pulse could've held out when he poured on the charm, and she'd caved. Within six months she'd fallen helplessly in love with him, with his tenderness, his gentleness and the way he'd made her feel safe and cherished. The fact that he'd enough sexual energy to power up the lights at Candlestick Park hadn't hurt, either, she thought with a wry grin.

They'd moved in together within a year and midway through their final year of law school, they'd eloped. After graduation, they'd both worked as law clerks while awaiting bar results. Nolan had clerked for an appellate court judge and she'd been essentially downgraded from paralegal to law clerk at the legal aid office where she'd worked her last two semesters. Even after they'd both passed the bar exam, they'd been broke much of the time, but it hadn't made a difference because they'd been happy. Or so she'd believed, until her past had reared up and bitten her so hard she'd panicked.

Regardless of how much they had loved each other, in the end she'd known it would never be enough. Rather than face her fears, she'd pushed him away with the determination of a defensive lineman out to sack the quarterback. She couldn't blame Nolan, only herself, and she'd used the excuse of his accepting the job offer from Turner, Crawford and Lowe—one the state's largest law firms—without consulting her as the perfect excuse to pick a fight. Rather than trust him with the truth about her past and admit she'd been lying to him all along about who and what she was, she'd told him to get out and to never come back.

Her life had spiraled out of control shortly thereafter. To numb herself from the pain of losing Nolan, she'd open a bottle of bourbon and start drinking until she literally could feel no pain. But the hurt had kept coming back and so she'd kept drinking until, almost a year later, she didn't know how to stop.

One night after leaving a downtown bar at closing time, she'd made a serious mistake and climbed behind the wheel of her car. Luckily a cop had pulled her over before she'd driven more than a block from the parking lot and she thanked God she hadn't hurt anyone but herself. She'd jeopardized not only her life and the lives of anyone unfortunate enough to be on the road that night, but she'd risked her career and shattered any remaining hope she'd secretly harbored of a reconciliation with Nolan because she'd never wanted him to have to live with the shame of having an alcoholic for a wife.

Mortified by what she'd become, she'd driven the final stake through the heart of her marriage when she'd called Nolan to insist he fly down to Mexico for a quickie divorce. They'd argued fiercely several times, until she'd finally lied and said she didn't love him, that she didn't know if she ever really had, blaming him because she'd been too young when they'd married. She would've gone to Mexico herself, but she'd been unable to leave the state since the judge had ordered her into rehab and placed her on probation for two years.

Two days before she'd entered rehab, Nolan had finally agreed to the divorce. The next day she'd hired the first attorney from the border town of Mexicali willing to make an appearance on her behalf on such short notice. Nolan, luckily, never found out that his wife had become an alcoholic. Twenty-eight days later she'd returned to her apartment and a notarized copy of their dissolution had been waiting for her amid a stack of bills, junk mail and periodicals.

Mikki flicked a length of ash and blinked back the sudden moisture blurring her vision. Who would've thought after all this time tough-as-nails Mikki Correlli could still tear up at the thought of a failed marriage? Sure as hell not her. She no longer allowed her emotions to control her actions.

She hadn't always been so resilient. The truth was, if it hadn't been for her family, she honestly didn't know if she would've survived the aftermath of Nolan once she'd sobered up. When the strength she'd always prided herself on had come close to deserting her again, her sisters and mother were there for her, offering their support without judgment, even if they hadn't agreed with the choices she'd made.

The urge to go home suddenly hit her hard. Not to her cozy apartment in the Marina District, but to the comfort of her mom's place on Garrison Street near Haight and Ashbury.

Suddenly she craved the gentle scents of cinnamon candles and strawberry incense, the strains of the Grateful Dead, Joan Baez or the Doors lingering in the background. The solidity of the spindle-back oak chairs at the ancient oak table in the spacious kitchen decorated with chickens and roosters, where she could sit and sip one of her mom's specialty herb tea blends and regain a proper perspective of her own role in the universe.

Tonight she wanted to listen to Emma reminisce about Haight-Ashbury, the Summer of Love, how she had traveled across the country in a VW bus to Woodstock and about the Oregon commune she'd lived in and where Rory had been born. Maybe Mikki would get lucky and recapture her own sense of calm. Although, she thought with a teary smile, she did often wonder if Emma's always sage advice wasn't peppered by the occasional acid flashback. Emma had experienced a few wilder moments in her free-love, mind-expanding days.

Her smile faded the instant she sensed Nolan's presence behind her. Once again she wondered at his reason for returning to the city. The last she'd heard he'd been busy setting legal precedent in several landmark cases. Some rulings she had silently applauded, others she'd vehemently cursed when reading about them in the quarterly supplements to the *California Reporter*. Because she read the periodicals faithfully to familiarize herself with new decisions in regard to matters related to her area of expertise, it was difficult not to notice the Baylor name when it appeared with such regularity.

When he joined her, she quietly asked, "Why are you here, Nolan?"

Facing her, he rested his hand on the railing. He wore one of those rascal grins she'd always adored. "To unlock a few possibilities."

She didn't appreciate his humor. "I'm serious." Thank goodness the odds of that happening were one in at least two hundred and fifty. More, possibly, judging by the size of the crowd that had turned out to support Baxter House.

His grin deepened, as if he knew something she didn't. "So am I," he arrogantly countered.

Not comfortable with all that cocky self-assurance aimed at her, Mikki's defensiveness became more pronounced. "You never did know how to be serious."

The smile faded and he let out a rough sigh. He pushed off the railing. "Can we sheathe the claws for a while?" He moved closer, eliminating the distance between them. "I came to talk to you, not fight."

Unless she was prepared to climb over the thick round base of the planter to escape him, which she wasn't—yet, he'd managed to effectively corner her. "So, now you've seen me," she said with a careless shrug she had no hope of believing was real. "Curiosity satisfied?"

He swept the length of her with his gaze, his eyes lingering a moment too long on her breasts. The way he was blatantly staring at her with such unmistakable desire caused her nipples to bead and tighten.

Some things never changed.

"God, you look so good." He took the remains of the cigarette from her fingers and tossed it into the Pacific before gently dragging the back of his hand down her cheek.

The lump in her throat tripled in size.

"But," he added, his voice dropping to a low, husky timbre, "you always did."

Awareness stirred within her. She stared at his mouth. "So do you." The admission slipped out before she could stop herself. An overwhelming urge to kiss him gripped her—hard. She trembled.

He continued to hold her gaze as he tipped her face upward with the pad of his thumb. Anticipation sizzled between them. Just as it always had, she thought.

Slowly he lowered his head.

"Nolan." Her soft whisper sounded remarkably reminiscent of an invitation rather than a protest. And honest, she decided. Regardless of how insane and stupid it was, she wanted him to kiss her.

The first feathery brush of his lips against hers instantly ignited her senses, taking her by total surprise. She hadn't known what to expect, but she sure as hell hadn't counted on her heart pounding or her insides turning to mush from an overload of sexual excitement.

She really did know better. With Nolan, indifference ceased to exist. He'd always made her feel too much. Too much love. Too much anger. Too much passion. Too much pain.

Damn you.

When he settled his mouth more firmly over hers and

deepened the kiss, she tried to tell herself the only reason she responded, the only viable excuse for slipping her arms around his neck, stemmed from the shock of seeing him again. Clearly she wasn't capable of thinking straight. Under normal circumstances, she never would've dreamed of plastering herself against him.

But she did and he tugged her even closer. He pulled her into a tailspin of sensation no woman who prided herself on calling the shots would ever dare welcome— or tolerate.

God help her, it wasn't nearly enough.

In one step he had her up against the rough stucco wall, surrounding her with the heat of his body. Flaming, steamy memories flashed through her mind. His hands, his lips, the thick, hard length of him pulsing in her hands, in her mouth, thrusting relentlessly into her until the control she never could maintain with him shattered and she flew apart.

The insistent ache of desire dampened her. She wanted to recreate those memories with a desperation so fierce it left her as breathless as his hot, wet kiss.

No. She would not, could not, go there again. *Ever.* He was her drug of choice, her fix. She'd plummeted to rock bottom once and had barely survived the experience. There wasn't a chance in hell she'd risk that kind of pain again, not when she couldn't be certain she possessed enough strength to crawl back the next time.

With every last shred of willpower she could summon, she planted her palms firmly on his chest and shoved him away. "No." The command sounded as ragged as her breathing—and about as convincing. "This is not going to happen."

Not again. Not *ever* again.

He took a reluctant step back, jammed his fingers through his hair and stared at her. She found no comfort from the fact he appeared as shaken as her by the heat that had flared up so quickly between them.

She prayed for numbness. Her body continued to hum defiantly with desire.

Just one more in a long line of unanswered prayers, she thought cynically. As if she should be surprised.

"What do you want, Nolan?" she asked him again. Her terse question fell short of rudeness due to the distinct tremor lacing her voice. Her trembling hands didn't help much, either. "And I want an answer this time."

He scrubbed his hand down his face. The wariness in his expression immediately filled her with dread.

"Nolan?" Her apprehension climbed with each passing silent second. "What? What is it?"

"When was the last time you were in Mexico?"

She frowned. Carefully she reached for the half empty glass of soda she'd left on the ledge of the redwood railing. She'd rather have a cigarette. Better yet, a drink.

"I've never been there." He, on the other hand, had spent the requisite twenty-four hours south of the border, she thought, feeling the bite of old hostility and resentment for what she'd insisted on in the first place.

She shook her head. Holding him responsible when

she'd been the one to demand the fastest method possible to put an end to their marriage was hardly fair or reasonable. "Why?" she asked cautiously.

"You never filed for a legal name change, either, did you?"

Icy cold fingers of panic slid around her throat and squeezed, threatening her air supply. "No," she managed to say in a choked whisper. "There wasn't any need to. You know that."

She'd refused to take his name once they'd married, which had infuriated him. But she'd refused to budge on the issue, so he'd eventually conceded defeat, albeit with massive reluctance. Although he'd never brought the subject up again, he'd made no secret of the fact that he wasn't happy with her decision to keep her own name. She hadn't needed some antiquated tradition of assuming her husband's name to know she was married, but in reality, as long as she kept her own name, she knew she'd never forget who or what she was—a Correlli. Not that she really held an ounce of admiration for her lineage, but she couldn't allow herself the false sense of security of the Baylor name.

He didn't say anything, just kept looking at her expectantly…waiting for her to put the pieces together. His eyes held everything she didn't want to know.

"Oh, God. We're not still…"

No, no, no. Not possible. Life could not be that cruel, could it?

"Married?" he finished for her.

She nodded because she didn't believe herself capable of more than insane babbling.

A wry grin tipped his mouth. "Next time you hire a lawyer, Mikki, a word of advice—" he bent forward until they were practically nose to nose "—make sure he hasn't been disbarred first."

3

"DISBARRED! Are you sure?"

Mikki's stomach bottomed out at Nolan's slow, confirming nod. Surely they couldn't still be legally married.

"Why? But how? After all this time?"

They just *couldn't* still be married.

He nodded again. "I'm sure, Mikki."

"No," she said firmly, as if the small word had the power to erase the truth from his eyes. "It isn't possible."

"If it's any consolation," he said, "I was just as floored by the news."

"Floored" hardly came close. Dumbstruck, blindsided and bewildered were more apt descriptions for the shock of the blow he'd just delivered. She felt as if she'd been sucker-punched. By a gorilla.

"Some consolation," she complained. She almost wished she hadn't pushed him away. An overload of sexual excitement, even with the wrong man, was better than hearing the news he'd just given her. "Why am I only finding out about this now?"

"Probably because the lawyer you hired didn't bother to mention he'd been disbarred about a week before you retained him." His voice was the epitome of calm.

She wanted to scream.

"But…how? Why?"

"The California State Bar Association takes issue with lawyers who play fast and loose with client trust accounts."

He leaned toward her again. His expression filled with a familiar challenge. "If you had taken my name like I wanted you to, the court clerk's office would've notified us when you filed a name change that your attorney was no longer legally permitted to practice. All this would have been avoided."

A lightening-hot flash of anger cut through the hazy fog in her brain. He was blaming her?

"So this is all my fault, is that it?" she fired at him, her voice rising. Okay, so maybe he did have a point, but she hadn't exactly been lucid at the time, either. If she'd been capable of doing so, she would've gone to Mexico herself and they wouldn't be having this insane conversation.

Nolan straightened and rammed his fingers through his wind-tossed hair for the second time. His dark brown eyes glowed with irritation.

Some things never changed, she thought again.

"I didn't say that," he said tightly.

No, he hadn't. She'd jumped to that conclusion all on her own. She understood her irrational reaction stemmed from the emotional bomb he'd just blasted her with, but that didn't give her the right to be so bitchy toward him. She'd been the one to retain a disbarred attorney, not him.

She let out a slow breath that provided zero calming effect and looked up at Nolan. Her husband?

Some things *really* never changed.

Oh, God.

"I'm sorry." She pressed her fingertips to her temple, hoping to relieve the pounding of what promised to be one nasty tension headache. "It's the shock."

He accepted her apology with a brusque nod.

Why was this happening? Suffering through the humiliation of another divorce proceeding, even if it were nothing more than a necessary technicality to legally end their marriage, wasn't something she relished facing. Admitting failure once should be enough punishment for anyone. Even her.

"How did you find out that we're still…" She couldn't bring herself to utter the word she'd evicted from her vocabulary the night she'd told him to leave. Right along with love, forever and all that happily-ever-after bullshit. Especially when she should've known better than to believe in any of it.

"Married." He completed the sentence for her, his tone wry. "Say it, Mikki. You won't choke on it."

"Wanna bet?"

A fresh wave of couples flooded onto the deck, drowning out the sound of his warm chuckle. After a quick glance over his shoulder, he narrowed the small space that separated them. Rather than reveling in the illusion of privacy, she felt as exposed and raw as the night she'd sent him packing.

"Well?" she prompted, tucking away yet one more unpleasant memory. Her specialty. "Why are we only learning about this now?"

He let out a sigh. "I found out during a routine background check." He kept his voice low so they wouldn't be overheard by the growing crowd. "It's firm policy for all partnership candidates under consideration."

Nolan? A partner? A stuffed shirt more interested in the bottom line than the complexities of the law? His last name might be Baylor, but her soon-to-be-again former husband hadn't ever been the least bit conservative. Although he easily had the arrogance market cornered, she thought derisively.

"You're joking, right?"

He frowned, his expression once again framed in irritation. "Is that really so hard for you to believe?"

She folded her arms. "Actually, yes," she said uncharitably.

His lips thinned.

Guilt immediately pricked her conscience and she let out a long sigh. Why did they always bring out the worst in each other? Couldn't they, just once, have a civilized conversation without going for the short hairs? Better yet, why couldn't she at least pretend to behave like a logical, rational adult around him?

Because, she thought, when it came to Nolan, there was nothing reasonable about the way he made her feel. Around him, every emotion, each response, became magnified with brilliant intensity. Whether five or fifty years had passed, she doubted that aspect of her life would ever change.

The throbbing in her temple increased, the tempo sliding right into a double-time staccato of pain. "I'm sorry." She apologized—again. "It's just that you never were all that…"

"Serious?" He tucked his hands into the pockets of his trousers. His frown remained in place. "So you've said before."

She inwardly winced at the reminder, but could he really blame her? They'd once had their electricity shut off for a weekend because they'd come up short that month and hadn't been able to cover all of their expenses. Nolan hadn't been all that concerned, whereas she'd freaked. Her need for security and stability clashed with his go-with-the-flow methodology. She planned. Nolan never thought beyond the moment. A miserable combination that had been destined for disaster.

"People do change, Mikki," he said quietly.

Not in her experience. Her caseload alone supported her belief. Every abused, neglected or abandoned kid she represented was more than enough of a reminder that very few people possessed the strength to turn their lives around and keep them that way. The best she ever hoped for was a safe place for her juvenile clients, away from their abusers or their addicted parents who cared more about their next high than their own children. If she could convince the family court judges and social workers to place the child in the home of someone who at least provided an illusion of caring, then she considered the case a victory.

Oh yeah, people changed, all right…just not anyone she knew.

So what if Nolan had miraculously matured in the years they'd been apart? They would still be all wrong for each other. And she'd do well to remember that, too, and not the way he'd kissed her, as if he'd missed her as much as she'd missed him.

Exhibiting no willpower whatsoever, her gaze zeroed in on his mouth. Just because she'd responded to that kiss didn't mean a damned thing. Well, she amended, except for a poorly timed reminder that she hadn't had noteworthy sex in a while.

Now there was an area where she and Nolan had been incredibly compatible. And then some. The passion between them had always burned hot. Definite chemistry, the combustible kind. Despite the passage of time, from one little ol' kiss, she didn't doubt for a second that making love to him would be nothing short of pure perfection.

And damned satisfying, she silently added.

"Why are you here, Nolan?" she asked bluntly, anxious to tamp down the treacherous trail of her thoughts. "Surely you didn't come all the way to San Francisco just to tell me our divorce isn't legal when a letter from your attorney would have been sufficient."

"I've moved back."

Dread settled in her stomach like a lead weight. "Back?" she exclaimed, uncertain which had her more stunned—the news they were still married or that he'd returned to San Francisco.

To her dismay he nodded. "To San Francisco."

"Why?" she blurted. *Why* here *of all places?*

"I transferred from the L.A. office."

"California's a big state, Nolan. Couldn't you have transferred to San Diego or Ventura?" she asked desperately.

"I'm needed here."

Well she sure as hell didn't need, or want, him *here*. She'd worked too hard to get over him. Odds were, since they both practiced family law, they were bound to eventually stumble over each other in the courtroom, either opposing each other or perhaps even on the same side, but that made little difference. Her reaction to that stupid kiss was more than enough reason for her to want to keep her distance.

It doesn't matter.

The reminder fell sadly short and she knew it. It didn't matter that she was supposed to have stopped loving Nolan ages ago. Where he lived, worked, his interests, none of it was supposed to make a bit of difference to her.

It doesn't matter.

He could move into one of the first-floor units of her building for all she cared. She wasn't supposed to give a damn.

It doesn't matter.

Only, it did matter. Dammit, *he* mattered—a hel-luva lot more than he should.

While she struggled to digest the fact that Nolan had actually returned to San Francisco for good, he reached into his pocket and withdrew the small white-gold key she'd seen him with earlier. She gave serious consideration to taking a flying leap over the railing and diving headfirst into the frigid ocean below. With the way her luck had turned tonight, risking her neck had to be the lesser evil.

A scoundrel's grin curved his lips as he reached for the locket around her neck.

She swatted his hand. "What do you think you're doing?"

"What does it look like?"

As though he was about to turn her life even more upside down. She attempted to take a step back, but the stucco wall behind her prevented a clean getaway. Now would be an excellent time to take that hike over the planter.

Undeterred, his long fingers brushed against the slope of her breast as he lifted the small trinket. His smile turned downright devilish. "What do you say we test our luck?"

"Not even fate can have that much of a sense of humor." No way in hell was she going on a date with Nolan. She'd drink antifreeze first.

Her breath caught. The soft click of the key unlocking the fourteen-karat miniature suitcase sealed her fate.

She should've taken her chances with the Pacific.

His reckless, heart-stopping grin deepened. "What are the odds?" He laughed, as if he'd known all along he held the key to her locket.

"They were supposed to be one in a few hundred." It didn't take a degree in rocket science for her to realize Nolan was the significant contributor Maureen had mentioned, or that she'd been sold out by one of her closest friends, even if it was for a good cause.

He gave a careless shrug, then shook the tiny numbered ticket inside the equally small suitcase loose. "Lucky me, then."

And unlucky her.

"Shall we claim our prize?"

"Not so fast." She snagged the ticket from his fingers. "I'll be claiming this prize. On my own." She gave him the hard stare she'd perfected. A lesser man would've bolted for the nearest exit. Nolan remained unfazed. "After the shock you've given me tonight, I've earned it."

Desperate for distance, she shouldered past him. She wanted time to think, to assimilate and analyze all that had occurred tonight. Needed time to develop a foolproof game plan.

She needed a drink. *Now.*

Nolan's big warm hands settled over her shoulders, halting her escape. "You deserve a lot more than some cheesy raffle prize." He dragged his thumbs rhythmically over her bare shoulders. "Much more than I was capable of—then."

She wasn't going anywhere near that comment. Not when she had gooseflesh puckering all over her skin from his touch and her nipples had hardened into tight peaks.

"Let me go, Nolan."

He didn't. "I can make it up to you, Mikki."

His warm breath fanned her ear. The heat of his body warmed her back. She closed her eyes. If only…

"If you'll let me," he whispered.

Her eyes flew open. Let him break her heart again? Not a chance. No way would she become one of those pathetic women who continue to make the same mistakes with the same wrong guy, over and over. *They* were over.

She pulled away, then shot him a scathing look over her shoulder. "You can start by filing an ex parte application. Get the court to agree to shorten the time or waive notice for a hearing so we file a motion to have our divorce recognized. Either that, or we go back to Mexico and get it right this time."

He tucked his hands into the pockets of his dark trousers again. "I doubt it will be that simple."

As much as she hated to admit it, he was right. When it came to their relationship, there never had been anything simple about it.

"You're a good lawyer, Nolan. Make it happen." Without waiting for a reply, she escaped through the double doors and practically jogged to the bar.

God, she needed a drink. No, she amended, sidling up to the polished length of mahogany. She didn't need a drink, she needed to erase the memories the only way she knew how.

She signaled for the bartender, but he was busy serving other customers and didn't see her. Maybe she should take that as a sign to put as much distance as possible between herself and temptation.

She slid onto a vacant bar stool.

Just to think, she reminded herself. She needed time to pull it together before she blew four of the toughest years of her life with a shot of Jack Daniel's.

She toyed with the catch on her evening bag, but each scrape of her thumbnail against the gold-plated clasp only echoed the gnawing desire for a drink until she thought she'd crawl out of her skin. Her hands trembled, so she fisted them in her lap, digging her nails into her palms, but the craving refused to ebb.

One shot of Old Number Seven. Only one, she thought, imaging the first splash from the square, black-labeled bottle of Kentucky bourbon filling a shot glass. The sweet, potent aroma as she lifted the glass to her lips. The trail of liquid fire down her throat...

The numbness. The ultimate escape into nothingness.

"What can I get you?"

"Double bourbon. Straight up," she told the bartender before her conscience could stop her. "And keep them coming."

Mikki squeezed her eyes shut, fearing the wrecking ball slamming against her brain would start up again if

she risked opening them. The hangover from hell had
arrived in full blown glory. As much as she would've
loved to hold Nolan responsible, he hadn't been the one
to pour all those double bourbons down her throat.

Slowly she opened her eyes, remembering to shield
them from the harsh glare of brilliant sunlight stream-
ing through the row of windows in her bedroom. She
attempted to ease toward the edge of the bed, but a sudden unexpected piercing pain in her in hip jarred her.

She flopped back against the pillows and let out a
groan. The pounding in her head momentarily intensi-
fied. She attempted slow, even breaths until the pain
subsided. When that failed, she muttered a string of
curses.

What the hell had she done?

Aside from the excellent job of becoming so thoroughly wasted Rory had not only had to drive her home
but had apparently had to help her up the stairs to her
apartment. When Mikki screwed up, she did a good job
of it. She couldn't even be certain Rory had been the
one to bring her home. Maybe it was Lauren? No, definitely Rory.

Exercising an abundance of caution, she eased herself up from the bed, then limped toward the bathroom
where she stripped off her panties and an old battered
Berkeley Law School T-shirt she hadn't worn in years.
Obviously, Rory's caretaking hadn't ended with depos-
iting her inside her apartment, because Mikki would
never have slept in a shirt Nolan had left behind unless
she'd been completely blitzed out of her mind.

Oh, wait. She *had* been blitzed out of her mind, she thought with a hefty dose of self-loathing. Of all the stupid things she'd ever done, ordering that first drink beat them all.

Regret, disgust and shame slammed into her simultaneously. She stumbled and reached for the sink to steady herself. With one act of sheer stupidity, she'd obliterated every stride she'd made in cleaning up and staying that way. Not once in four years had she slipped—and she'd been close plenty. One hour in Nolan's presence and look at her...she had mother of a hangover, unaccountable bruises and no one to blame but her own weak self.

Before she thought better of it, she held the T-shirt to her face and breathed in, but the tangy citrus aroma she remembered so well had long been washed away. Closing her eyes, she inhaled more deeply. Her olfactory senses didn't require a jolt for the images to instantly flicker through her mind with haunting familiarity. The intensity in Nolan's rich brown eyes as he made love to her... Her hands smoothing over the hard, sleek surface of his skin... Touching. Tasting. Reacquainting herself with the unforgettable contours of his body.

She and Nolan might have a serious communication problem, but that didn't mean they didn't speak with perfect clarity in bed. She rubbed the soft, worn fabric against her cheek and remembered. Nolan beneath her as she eased her body over his long, thick length. His hands cupping her bottom, coaxing, urging her take all of him inside her. His body thrusting upward to meet hers, filling her and driving her to the point of total mindlessness. Sexually, they'd been ravenous, completely demanding, neither willing to settle for anything less than the other's soul.

In her mind she heard his deep-throated groans mingle amid the erotic words of encouragement he whispered to her. She imagined how he would push her to lose control and her cries as passion claimed them, leaving them spent and thoroughly sated.

Her eyes flew open and she tossed the T-shirt to the floor in disgust. How stupid was she? Apparently a whole lot more than she gave herself credit for being if she willingly wandered into the danger zone. What was next? Mimosas for breakfast?

In a fit of temper, she slammed the bathroom door, regretting the act of immaturity the instant the loud crack reverberated through her throbbing skull. In the full-length mirror, she examined the dark, ugly bruise on her hip and not the silly, useless daydreams that got her into trouble. Nolan might be back in town, but that didn't mean she'd be inviting him back into her bed anytime soon. That much of a masochist she wasn't.

Gingerly she pressed her fingers against the bruised flesh above her hipbone. She winced from the flash of pain. Another smaller bruise just above her left knee looked no better than the purplish-blue stain on her hip. A quick press of her fingers against the offensive spot quickly confirmed it felt as bad as it looked.

Why? she asked herself. She'd fought off cravings before. Why hadn't she managed to control herself last night?

"Because you're weak, that's why."

Because that first taste of Jack Daniel's had been too damned good.

She took a good long look at her reflection. Disgusted with herself, she let out a low-pitched hiss of utter loathing.

She'd really done it this time. Her hair looked as if it were good for nothing more than a habitat for sewer rats. Dark smudges of mascara underscored her bloodshot eyes, doing nothing to complement the ghastly paleness of her complexion. Although the realization that she'd thrown four years of sobriety away sickened her, if all she had were a few unaccountable bruises and a hangover, she should count herself lucky. The last time she'd drunk herself into a blackout, she'd ended up in a jail cell and facing possible disbarment.

A shudder passed over her at the reminder and she quickly turned on the shower. She knew what she had to do—start over with the first step of day one in a long, arduous process—to avoid ending up in the same horrid condition tomorrow morning.

Once the water heated, she carefully stepped beneath the stinging spray. Drinking herself into oblivion to the point where she had no recollection of what she'd done, and that she could go there again so quickly, scared the hell out of her. She wasn't proud of her actions, but she possessed enough self-awareness to realize that if she didn't stop berating herself, she'd likely end up in some bar with a drink in her hand before sunset.

The trouble with drinking away problems was they were still present the morning after. Numbness, unfortunately, was only a temporary cure, one with nasty side effects.

At least when Nolan escaped from reality, he didn't dive into the nearest shot glass. No, she thought, he moved away.

Twenty minutes later she emerged from the bathroom, her physical condition at least marginally improved. Her emotional state required more than hot water and melon-scented bath gel. But the aches in her body had lessened a degree or two, even if she couldn't say the same for her disposition or the horrendous pounding in her head, something combing the fierce tangles from her hair had only amplified. Coffee and a dose of extra-strength aspirin would hopefully provide much-needed relief from the pain. Too bad the over-the-counter remedy wouldn't eradicate the pain she'd escaped for a few drunken hours.

But a little hair of the dog sure as hell would.

She let out a stream of breath, determined to ignore that particular desire and to concentrate on dressing. The time had long passed for her to meet her sisters for their Saturday morning bull session. Since she had no plans to leave her apartment until she felt slightly more human, she opted for maximum comfort. Besides, she didn't exactly look forward to facing her sisters until she managed to pull herself back together. As much as she'd rather hide out in the sanctity of her apartment for the entire weekend, she knew she'd have to leave the apartment eventually. For now, she pulled on a loose-fitting pair of faded army pants she'd picked up at the local surplus store, then paired them with a buttery soft, long-sleeved ivory T-shirt.

She left the bedroom and walked directly into the living room, immediately greeted by the tantalizing aroma of freshly brewed coffee and what she'd wager were warm croissants from Rory's. She heard a drawer open, followed by the clatter of silverware, and managed a thin smile despite her shame.

Circling the back of the navy corduroy sofa, she crossed the hardwood floor of the living room in her bare feet to the microscopic-size kitchen. Although prepared to pledge her eternal gratitude, she couldn't help but be curious about her sister going to so much trouble for her after last night.

She paused. Unless she'd been in worse shape than she imagined. Although Rory's unexpected presence on what historically marked the busiest day of the week at Lavender Field stemmed from concern, Mikki was in no mood for a well-meaning, albeit deserved, lecture. Although she had little to no recollection of the previous night, she didn't doubt for a second that Rory and Lauren were disappointed in her.

"If those are croissants I smell, then this qualifies as above and beyond the call of sisterhood," she called. "Not that I'm about to—"

Mikki rounded the corner and stopped cold.

She stared in total astonishment, not at Rory, but at the last person she'd ever expected—and hoped never—to see in her apartment.

"Complain?" Nolan finished her sentence, just as he'd always done. "That's a relief." His grin turned mildly sheepish. "After last night, I wasn't sure you'd be all that pleased to see me."

4

NOW WHAT had she done?

"Last night?" She despised the apprehension in her voice almost as much as the fact that she felt compelled to even ask the question. Worse, she hated what she could possibly be revealing to Nolan—that he'd rattled her to the point she'd done the unthinkable and plowed through several shot glasses of bourbon.

Following their rendezvous beneath the stars, her evening had become an alcohol-induced blur. Worse than a blur, she amended. A blackout.

She wasn't fooled by his casual shrug. The concern she easily detected in his gaze told her he saw right through her hangover to the truth. That she couldn't remember a damned thing.

He retrieved an oversize Lavender Field mug from the cabinet by the sink, then filled it with coffee. "Stranger things have happened," he said easily.

"Thanks." She automatically took the mug he offered and wrapped her fingers around the warmth of the ceramic. "Uh…do you mind telling me exactly what did happen?"

She took a tentative sip. Strong and black, just the way she liked it. Therein lay her problem. Nolan knew exactly how she liked...*everything*.

His gaze dipped to her breasts, her diamond-hard nipples evident beneath the shirt clinging to her, but he turned away without comment or that all-too-knowing grin she'd expected. She'd thought he'd disappeared after she'd left him last night, but what if he'd hung around the bar long enough to witness her pounding shots like a professional barfly? Would the revelation that she was capable of drinking herself into oblivion shock him or finally clue him in to the signs she'd miraculously kept hidden during their marriage? Control had always been, and still was, too important to her, and until he'd left, she had managed to keep a tight rein on the overwhelmingly growing desire to drink. Sure, they'd both indulged occasionally, the only difference was, she hadn't stopped until she'd been beyond wasted. She'd drank socially—right into oblivion.

Last night he'd implied he'd changed. What would he say about the changes in her? Only in her case, change and improvement weren't necessarily synonymous.

"Just so we're on the same page," she started as nonchalantly as possible, despite her reservations, "what 'stranger things' were you referring to?"

He opened the fridge for a carton of milk and poured a splash into a matching mug. "The news about our divorce not being legal."

The oven timer dinged. After returning the milk to

the fridge, he slid a baking sheet laden with light, flaky croissants from the oven.

"Are those from Rory's?" she asked, breathing in the familiar aroma.

His nod confirmed her suspicions. She really shouldn't be surprised, but she couldn't help but feel the minute sting of sisterly betrayal just the same. Her family adored Nolan, her mom and sisters had always doted on the guy. Who could blame them? He possessed an uncanny charm capable of melting even her reserve. His being armed with croissants from Rory's shop told her he'd already sweet-talked his way right back into Rory's good graces.

The kitchen lacked decent counter space, so he set the baking sheet on top of the burners of the small stove before he cast a curious glance her way. "Why?" he asked, sounding almost bored. "What did you think I meant?"

She wasn't buying his blasé routine for a second. The man knew far too much about her already, which irritated her as much as her inability to recall if she'd even spoken to him after she'd left him on the deck at Clementine's.

She concentrated on taking another sip from the mug. "Nothing." She added a shrug for good measure. "It's not important."

A surreptitious glance in his direction revealed a half smile she considered far too smug playing across her husband's mouth. *Ex*-husband, she corrected, then gritted her teeth.

Why didn't he just come right out and ask her what he wanted to know? Instead, he continued to goad her into playing some stupid game. All he had to do was take one good look into her bloodshot eyes to realize that in her current condition he held a distinct advantage over her.

He carried the plate of pastries over to the maple drop-leaf table situated beneath the pair of tall windows. "Come and eat while they're hot." He returned to the fridge for sliced melon and a jar of raspberry preserves. The man was nothing if not prepared.

She dragged a chair out and sat. "Fine. You win. I admit it," she said irritably. "I had too much to drink last night." She set her mug on the table with a thwack loud enough to start her head thumping again. "My memory is a little fuzzy this morning. Satisfied?"

He set a white ceramic bowl of chilled melon chunks on the table and looked at her. A predatory gleam entered his chocolate-colored eyes, exciting her in a flash. "Satisfaction never was a question between us," he reminded her.

The overstuffed-cotton feeling in her head prevented any hope of a snappy comeback. Or was it the sexier-than-sin cant of his mouth as he braced his hand on the back of her chair and leaned in close, leaving her feeling stupid and tongue-tied? Did it even matter?

She didn't think so. Not when all she could think about was how if she tilted her head just a tiny fraction to the right, they'd be in perfect alignment for one of those bone-melting kisses hot enough to reduce her to ash.

Great. More temptation she didn't need to deal with at the moment.

"I didn't realize we were having a contest," he continued smoothly. "But if you're already conceding defeat, then how about giving me my prize?"

God help her, she wanted him to kiss her. She wanted it so badly, if he didn't, she just might.

She didn't know which was more distracting—Nolan and the seductive combination of his own alluring male scent mingled with his citrus aftershave, or the warmed rolls from Lavender Field. For that matter, she wasn't sure which held more appeal—giving in to the fantasy of that hot wet kiss, or the buttery baked goods. Either indulgence was bad for her, but since when had that ever stopped her?

Suddenly ravenous, she tiled her head a fraction to the right...then snagged a roll from the plate. It was much easier to shed pounds than to mend a broken heart—again.

"Stop it, Nolan." The warning fell flat thanks to the noticeable trembling of her hand as she smeared a pat of butter over the croissant. Thankfully her voice remained steady. "I'm not in the mood for your crap this morning."

He took his sweet time backing off and eventually let out a sigh. "You really don't remember last night?" he asked, taking the seat opposite her.

"Oh, I remember enough," she said, electing to ignore the underlying accusation in his tone. "How could I not? Finding out your ex *isn't?* Not quite what I'd call an unforgettable moment." She gave him a saccharine smile. "Unfortunately."

He shot her a look of tempered patience. "Give it a few days. You'll get used to the idea."

"Don't hold your breath, Baylor," she said, and made a sound of disgust he'd have to be dense to mistake as complimentary. She scooted her chair back, the legs scraping loudly across the linoleum. "We won't be staying married long enough for *that* to happen."

He spooned a few chunks of melon onto his plate. "I didn't come here to pick a fight with you, Mikki," he said wearily.

"Then why are you here? I haven't seen or heard from you in years and yet in the past twelve hours, you've become the equivalent of bad cold."

"Since when is having breakfast with my wife a crime?"

"*Ex*-wife," she corrected hotly. She stalked to the cabinet near the sink where she kept the aspirin and shook three from the bottle before returning to the table. "And while we're on the subject—" she popped the aspirin in her mouth and chugged them down with lukewarm coffee "—you of all people should know breaking and entering *is* a crime."

He had the audacity to lean back in his chair and flash her one of his high-voltage smiles. "Really? How you figure?"

Too restless to sit, she drained the last of her coffee and returned for a refill. "Maybe because this is *my* apartment and I don't recall issuing *you* an invitation."

"But you don't know that for certain, now do you?"

The smug taunt wiped out her appetite. Dammit, she hated it when he was right.

"Don't you dare use me to perfect your cross-examination skills, Nolan. What I know or don't know stopped being your concern a long time ago." Feeling way too defensive in front of him, she set the cup behind her on the counter so hard coffee sloshed over the rim, seeping into the grout. Crossing her arms, she gave him a good, hard stare. "I'd appreciate it if you'd leave."

He stood, and for two seconds she believed her luck might actually have changed. Her relief was short-lived, however. Rather than bolt for the door like the rest of his kind whenever she pulled the prickly bitch routine, he walked purposely toward her, that predatory gleam back in his eyes.

Her pulse revved.

"So I'm not welcome in my own home, is that it?" The amusement in his voice was really starting to tick her off.

"Your home? Where do you get off—"

He pulled a ring of keys from the pocket of his dark blue trousers and dangled them in front of her.

Disbelief rippled through her. "You still have a key?" she asked incredulously.

The ring slid across the counter when he tossed them on the ceramic tiles. "If you didn't want me to come back, then you should've changed the locks."

She'd take amusement over that all-too-knowing smile of his any day. Especially when all she could think about were long, deep kisses.

He was too close—to her and to the truth. "Why? You were never coming back." She aimed for sarcastic, but landed in the middle of hurt not even five years of separation could completely diminish.

As if he sensed her pain, he cupped her cheek in the warmth of his palm. "Never say never," he said gently, then brushed his mouth lightly over hers.

Varying degrees of need instantly demanded attention. The deep keening need to kiss him back, the desperate desire to put as much distance as possible between them. Regardless of how ridiculous, she still wanted to wrap her arms around him and hold on tight so he'd never be able to leave her again. Better yet, she could drag him into the bedroom and make love to him for hours. Wild, hot sex the way they used to…

Enough already.

A smart woman wouldn't so much as consider acting on such foolish impulses. When it came to Nolan, hadn't she fulfilled her quota of mistakes for a lifetime?

Obviously not.

Dammit, she knew better than to play games she couldn't win, but that didn't stop her from slipping her arms around his neck and slanting her mouth beneath his, taking the kiss from tentative and light to deep and soul-reaching. His hands settled on her waist, his fingers dipping beneath the band of her loose-fitting army pants to press into the flesh of her bottom. He hauled her up against him, obliterating her common sense.

The heavy beat of her heart drowned out the pounding in her head. Her body came vibrantly alive under his touch and she pressed even closer, loving the feel of him against her, wanting to feel the weight of him above her, needing to feel the heat and length of him inside her.

His hands roved her curves, pushing up her shirt to expose her breasts. Cool air brushed her heated skin. His lips left hers and at his sharp intake of breath, her eyes drifted closed and her head fell back. The heat of his mouth closed over her nipple, dragging a moan from her throat. Heat pooled in her belly. The musky scent of her arousal rose around them like steam from a hot tub on a cold, brisk night.

She dug her nails into Nolan's wide shoulders as a tiny wave of pleasure unexpectedly rocked her, leaving her shaken yet hungry for more. She wanted him inside her, filling her, loving her…

What was wrong with her? The man wasn't only capable of breaking her heart, but one night in his presence and he'd unwittingly shattered her carefully reconstructed existence. Hadn't drinking herself into a blackout last night proven anything?

She opened her eyes and pushed him away. "Ever hear the one about you can't go home again?" As she tugged her top back into place, she prayed the old saw applied to ex-husbands and bedrooms, else she was in serious trouble. If his mere touch had her body so amped up with sizzling desire, making love to him would throw her into the equivalent of a nuclear meltdown.

Yeah, but what a way to go.

His hands settled on her upper arms. "I never did put much stock in clichés," he said, skimming his palms down to her hands to lace their fingers together.

"We *are* a bad cliché." She couldn't do this. She didn't have that much strength.

She tugged free and wrapped her arms around her middle. "What do you want, Nolan? Or did you come here just to play games?"

He had the audacity to smile.

Lethal. No other description fit the deepening of his grin when he planted his hands on the counter and surrounded her.

"Looks to me as if we'd still be damned good at certain games."

His sexy implication stoked the smoldering embers of her far-too-easily-ignited libido. Her nipples throbbed, aching for more of his touch. Desire continued to tug insistently at her belly.

Damn him.

"Forget it." She was doing enough thinking about *that* for both of them.

"I've thought of little else since last night." His voice settled into low sexy timbre she easily recognized as the erotic equivalent of a slow, familiar caress between lovers. And twice as effective.

"Nolan."

He ignored the distinct warning in her voice, his hand drifting to the side of her neck where he tenderly brushed her damp hair aside. "I want you, Mikki." He pressed the pad of this thumb lightly against the pulse beating rapidly at the base of her throat. "That hasn't changed."

Maybe not, but too much about her had. "Then I suggest a cold shower."

His smile turned even more devilish. She thought he'd never looked more handsome.

"Speaking from experience?" he asked with a hike of a single dark eyebrow.

If you only knew.

Somehow she managed a reasonable facsimile of a caustic laugh. She snagged her coffee, then brushed past him. "The only things that haven't changed are your arrogance and your inability to take anything seriously."

Distance was paramount to her survival. Otherwise she just might offer a more promising solution than a cold shower—such as finishing what they'd started.

He caught her by the waist before she managed a clean getaway. With a gentle tug, he pulled her against him. His arm banded her waist as he held her tight, aligning his body to hers.

She closed her eyes and absorbed the heat of his body against her back. Her hormones went flying into a tailspin. What little willpower she'd managed to summon earlier threatened to evaporate into the highly charged air surrounding them.

"Neither has the effect you still have on me."

Oh, God, on her, either. It'd always been that way between them. She wasn't stupid enough to believe for a nanosecond the passage of time would ever dim the sexual chemistry between them. Not when she'd just provided him with enough evidence to the contrary.

His breath fanned the side of her neck, sending tingles chasing down her spine. "If we'd been alone last night rather than at Clementine's, don't think for a minute we wouldn't have made love, Mikki. Even after everything we've been through, I can still make you hot with nothing more than a kiss."

"Last night was a fluke," she said stiffly, praying she sounded more indifferent than she felt. "You were the last person I expected to run into at Maureen's fundraiser. I was caught off guard, is all."

He nuzzled the side of her neck and chuckled. "Yeah? So what's your excuse now, sweetheart?"

Words failed her as his flattened palm slowly inched upward to her breasts, which had remained swelled and aching for his touch. His tongue circled the shell of her ear. "You're wet for me now," he whispered arrogantly. "So slick."

He swept his hand down her rib cage and over her hip where his fingers pressed into the soft flesh above the waistband of her pants. The tip of his middle finger inched around the front to tease the snap, sliding just beneath the band to flick the elastic edge of her panties.

"Your clit's throbbing, isn't it?" he said. "How do you want to come, Mikki? You want me to tongue you to an orgasm? Or do you want to ride me the way you used to?"

Her resistance wavered dangerously. She tightened her grip on the mug in her hand. "Stop it," she whispered without an ounce of conviction.

As usual, he ignored her demand, placing light kisses along the side of her neck, the line of her jaw. "I know you, Mikki. I know your body. We were good together. Once. We could be again."

No, they couldn't. Making love to Nolan would be nothing short of spectacular. She knew that, and her body quickened in anticipation, need simmering hotly in her veins. But no matter how tempting the offer, she also knew they couldn't stay in bed forever. Out of the bedroom they wouldn't last a week.

"*Once* being the operative word." Out of self-preservation, she pulled away from him, equally surprised and disappointed when he let her go. Putting as much distance between them as her tiny kitchen allowed, she turned and blasted him with her iciest glare.

"What did you expect after the bomb you dropped on me last night? I might have had a moment of vulnerability, but all you were was a willing body. Don't fool yourself into thinking even this has anything to do with you. You're just handy, is all." She walked to the doorway. As if he were nothing more important than an afterthought, she stopped to look back at him. "Oh, and by the way, thanks for—" she let her gaze roam his body "—breakfast. You can go now."

He let out a harsh breath. "Dammit, Mikki." His voice rose in frustration. "It's always the same old story with you, isn't it? Why do you insist on always pushing me away?"

Because I'm not strong enough to survive you a second time.

"Look, we wrote our ending a lifetime ago," she said coolly. "You know I've never been a fan of sequels. They're never as good as the original."

"Tell that to Freddie or Jason."

"My point exactly."

She left the kitchen and for the space of a heartbeat, considered disappearing into the bedroom. Fear that he'd follow her rather than take her departure as the end to an old, tired argument, kept her in the living room. Besides, with her body still humming, she wouldn't last if she had him within the vicinity of her bed.

Not trusting herself anywhere near an opportunity for a horizontal position, she curled up in the armchair by the bay window in the living room and tucked her feet beneath her. She snagged the television remote from the hand-painted end table and channel-surfed until she found a baseball game on ESPN. She pretended interest in the Oakland A's as they took the field at the top of the third inning.

Sounds from the kitchen as Nolan cleared away their breakfast drifted into the living room. The man couldn't take a hint if a house dropped on his head. That he hadn't left bothered her almost as much as the fact he still knew his way around her kitchen...as if he still belonged here.

After he'd moved out of the apartment, she should've, as well, if only to escape the memories. But her salary at the time hadn't afford her the luxury of giving up the rent-controlled apartment, so she'd stayed and compensated with another, more destructive means of escape until she hadn't been able to stop.

With the love and unconditional support of her family, regular attendance at AA meetings, the help of her sponsor and sheer determination, she'd managed to remain sober for four years. Last night's slip shattered her confidence in staying that way.

In her thousand-plus days of sobriety she'd have given her soul countless times for a drink, but she hadn't succumbed once to the raw, stark cravings. There'd been the time an unsympathetic judge had granted custody to the wrong parent despite her objections. She hadn't lost her footing then. When a familiar client's folder crossed her desk again, the child more emotionally and physically damaged than the last time, she hadn't gone running for the nearest happy hour. One hour with Nolan and she'd climbed on the Bourbon Express and hadn't stopped until she'd hit Blackout City.

Six weeks ago had been one of the worst. She'd nearly caved when word that one of her clients had been hospitalized again courtesy of an abusive stepfather. Because the injuries had been too extensive, the little redheaded four-year-old girl with mysterious soft gray eyes hadn't lived through the night. Mikki hadn't fallen off the wagon then, and that day had qualified as one of the toughest since she'd cleaned up her act.

Despite the disappointments of her job, she'd worked hard not to give in to the near-crippling cravings for something stronger than a soda. The strongest drink to pass her lips, until last night, had been a double-shot espresso, regardless of the all-too-often desperate need to anesthetize herself from the disenchantment of being a child advocate. That she'd given in to the demons last night with little hesitation was more than enough of a reminder that Nolan was bad news.

She glanced up from the television screen when Nolan finally emerged from the kitchen twenty minutes later. He hardly looked pleased with her, but that was his problem. She had more than enough of her own to worry about at the moment. Getting through the next five seconds without a drink being her top priority.

"Goodbye, Nolan."

"So that's it, then?" he asked, his tone sharp and clipped.

She shrugged. "That's it." It had to be.

He glanced down at the hardwood floor for a brief instant, then lifted his gaze back to hers. She refused to acknowledge the frustration and disappointment in his eyes. She'd made her decision.

He stared at her long and hard for a moment before he spoke. "For what it's worth, Mikki, I never wanted the divorce." He left, quietly closing the door behind him.

She let her head fall back against the cushion and sighed, wishing like hell for a shot of bourbon to add to her coffee.

MIKKI SNAGGED THE PHONE on the second ring. "Yeah?" she answered sharply. Her disposition hadn't improved in the two hours since Nolan's departure, and the Oakland A's trailing the Chicago White Sox by two runs at the bottom of the ninth wasn't helping.

"In a mood, are we?"

Mikki managed a rueful grin at her older sister's light, teasing tone. She settled back into the soft fullness of the dark blue sofa. "The A's are getting their butts kicked and I have the hangover from hell."

"I'm not surprised," Rory said. "About the hangover. Is it bad?"

Mikki appreciated her sister's sympathy, but there was still a little matter of loyalty. "Not as bad as awaking up to find Nolan in my apartment."

"Oh?"

She wasn't buying Rory's feigned-innocent routine. "As if you didn't know," she said, managing to pull off a heartfelt chuckle. "The croissants were delicious, by the way." She'd devoured three of them during the fifth inning when the A's had managed to tie up the score. "Thanks for sending them. Traitor."

Rory's laughter was warm and effectively soothing. "You're welcome. So?"

"So nothing." She wasn't ready to explain how she'd practically made love to Nolan in the kitchen this morning. "Where's my car?"

"Ask your husband."

"He's *not* my husband. Or he won't be for much longer if I have anything to say about it." She took a tentative sip of the ginger ale she'd discovered at the back of the fridge. A damned sorry excuse for the bourbon and cola she craved, but the smarter option. "What do you mean, ask Nolan?"

"He drove your car over to your place this morning."

Although her headache had finally waned, she

moved cautiously as she rose from the sofa to look out the bay window. She pushed aside the sheers and, sure enough, her red, sporty two-seater was parked downstairs in front of her building. She rested her forehead against the window frame. "He never mentioned it."

"You probably didn't give him a chance."

True, she hadn't. She'd been too busy getting all hot and bothered. Nolan or a drink. Both were equally bad for her, but that didn't stop her from wanting both.

She frowned suddenly on her return to the sofa. "Rory, you didn't tell him that I'm an..." God. She couldn't say the word aloud. How the hell was she supposed to acknowledge responsibility if she couldn't even say the word?

Not that what she did with her life had anything whatsoever to do with Nolan Baylor. She stopped being his concern ages ago. Still, she didn't want him knowing just how bad her drinking had gotten after he'd left.

"That you're a what?" Rory asked pointedly, her tone remarkably close to a scolding taunt.

Or Mikki's own conscience.

"Forget it," she said sharply. "My life is my business."

Rory let out a weary sigh.

"I'm sorry," Mikki said, instantly contrite for snapping at her sister. "You don't deserve to be on the receiving end of my bad mood because I screwed up royally last night. It's just been a rotten day and it's not even half over."

"Apology accepted." Rory, gracious as always.

Mikki didn't know what she'd do without her family. They were literally all she had in the world. Or was willing to acknowledge now that she'd discovered Nolan still met the legal requirement of "next of kin."

"For the record, I meant that my life is no longer Nolan's concern. There isn't any reason for him to know."

"It's your decision."

Mikki's frown deepened when a White Sox outfielder caught a fly, not because of the disapproval she detected in her sister's voice. Two outs and not a man on base. At least she wasn't the only one suffering from a crappy day. "But you disagree."

"You know I do. I disagree a lot about how you handled things with Nolan. He deserves to know the truth."

Mikki sighed. "I've already have enough guilt to swallow after what I did last night. I'm not up for a Nolan and Mikki postmortem today."

"All right," Rory said. "When you want to talk, you know where to find me."

"Thank you," she said, appreciative of Rory's compassionate nature and mildly surprised her sister had backed off so easily. "So, to blatantly change the subject, did Nolan happen to tell you he's moved back to San Francisco?"

"I heard about it," her sister answered. "You told me, Mikki. Last night. But you don't remember, do you?"

"Unfortunately, no." Mikki sank farther into the cushions. "This sucks, Rory. I can't believe I did this. You know how hard it's been."

"I know," she said sympathetically. "You just have to start over."

"Would you be crushed if I moved to Siberia?"

"Devastated. So would Mom and Lauren, by the way."

Mikki managed a small smile. "Damn," she said. "I guess that's out, then."

"Guess so. I'll bet Nolan wouldn't like it much."

Her smile faded and she let out an impatient breath. "That's his problem. Not mine." Anxious for another change of topic, she forced a more serene tone. "Did you see Lauren this morning? What happened to her last night?"

"I don't know," Rory said. "She never came by the shop, but there was a new entry in Lorelei's Blog about the fund-raiser. That girl has a wicked way with words."

Mikki laughed, and it felt good. She and Rory got a kick out of the blog diary Lauren wrote under the pseudonym of "Lorelei" for the *San Francisco Inside Out* Web site in addition to the print column she also contributed to the magazine.

"Any idea who she hooked up with?" she asked, curious. Lauren always called if she couldn't make their standing Saturday bull session at Lavender Field.

"Not a clue."

"What about you and Tucker?"

Mikki envisioned Rory tensing at the mention of Tucker Schulz. She heard a thud on the other end and guessed her sister was busy beating risen bread dough into submission.

"What about him?" Rory asked, sounding conveniently distracted.

"You are going, right?" She did recall something about Rory and Tuck having a matching lock and key and winning the grand prize at last night's fund-raiser, the all-inclusive weekend at the exclusive Painter's Cove Resort in Mendocino.

"I haven't decided."

Mikki scoffed at her sister's reluctance. Tuck was one hot guy and it was apparent, at least to Mikki, that he wasn't immune to Rory's many charms by any stretch of the imagination. "What's to decide? Mud baths, hot stone massages, a luxury suite for two."

"With a total stranger," Rory reminded her.

"No, with Tuck. Rory, he's one of the good guys." Mikki had known him for as long as she'd known Nolan, and while he'd never been short of feminine companionship, Tuck wasn't the type to lead a woman on, unlike the creep that had practically left her sister at the altar.

"I don't know…" Rory hesitated.

"Go," Mikki insisted.

Rory ignored the command and continued to unmercifully pound some poor baked good on her worktable.

"Did you hear me?"

"I'll think about it," her sister eventually conceded.

From Rory's stiff tone, Mikki figured that was about as close to a commitment as she would drag from her at the moment. She decided to drop the subject. For now. There would be ample opportunity to goad Rory into taking advantage of the weekend in Mendocino when they met at Emma's for brunch tomorrow. Maybe she'd even enlist Lauren and Mom in the cause.

After promising to call the minute she heard from Lauren and making plans for lunch later that week, she hung up the phone. The A's center fielder hit a line drive, but the White Sox were determined to win and rallied the ball to first, seconds before the runner made the base.

She muttered in disgust, then flipped off the set before dialing Lauren's number. Her sister's cheery voice directed her to leave a message. Never a fan of loose ends, Mikki hated not knowing what her little sister was up to, and knew it would nag her until she tracked down Lauren. A fabulous diversion, but unfortunately, her kid sister's antics would have to wait. She had other more pressing matters requiring her immediate attention, finalizing her divorce from Nolan at the top of her list. He was a loose end that could easily become a noose tightening around her neck if she wasn't careful, and she didn't plan on allowing that to happen.

She wasn't looking forward to facing yet another failure in her life, but she refused to let Nolan's reappearance send her on another downward spiral. The scars of hitting rock bottom the last time were still too real.

Ninety minutes later, seated on a metal folding chair in the appointed room in the basement of the Marina District's community center, Mikki stared down at the brown-speckled asphalt tiles praying for courage she suspected she'd not find waiting to be scooped up from the floor beneath her feet. With one final deep breath, she stood and walked to the makeshift podium at the front of the room.

"Hi," she said to small crowd of approximately two dozen in attendance late on a Saturday afternoon. People just like her. She looked at each of the strangers in the room and was overcome by the instant bond she felt with them. There were no separations by gender, economic status or ethnicity. Addiction was an equal opportunity disease. Every person in the room shared some level of guilt, shame and regret for succumbing to the uncontrollable lure of whatever vice provided comfort to them. She took strength from them, safe in the knowledge that whomever stood up next to share their story, would do the same.

She cleared her throat and even managed a tentative smile. "Hi, she said again with more confidence. "My name is Mikki, and I'm an alcoholic."

5

NOLAN SLIPPED THE yellow legal pad inside the press-board folder, then leaned back into the soft Italian leather executive chair, stretching his arms above his head to help ease the stiffness from his back and neck. The grandfather clock at the far end of the formal study chimed the hour, followed by nine ominous-sounding bell tones. No wonder his back felt tight. He'd been working on the Delaney custody file for nearly four hours.

After leaving Mikki's around noon, he'd headed for the office intending to catch up on a few matters requiring his attention, only to have his plans preempted by the discovery of a new case his assistant had left on his desk marked "priority." The firm had only substituted into the case as of Friday, leaving him little time to familiarize himself with the facts or to prepare for the hearing on an injunction scheduled for Monday afternoon. Under the circumstances, he was almost grateful Mikki had blown him off that morning.

Almost, but not quite.

Convinced he'd lost every last shred of common

sense, he smiled ruefully and shook his head. Perhaps he did suffer from masochistic tendencies, as Tuck had suggested, because any relationship with Mikki sure as hell wouldn't make his life easier. Despite that knowledge, he still couldn't rid himself of the insane idea that just *maybe* this time around they could make a go of it. They were both older, hopefully a little wiser and, with any luck, smart enough not to make the same mistakes twice. But the truth was, he'd never stopped loving Mikki and doubted he ever would. From the moment he first saw her, he hadn't been able to stop thinking about her, and that, he understood, was just a fact of his life.

Time, he thought, closing the file. He doubted enough existed to weaken the explosive chemistry between them. Her response to him last night and again this morning, before she'd gone all prickly, proved his argument beyond a reasonable doubt. God knew he sure couldn't keep his hands off her. Although she'd told him to get lost, he suspected her refusal to admit she still wanted him was nothing short of a defense mechanism.

Or maybe she was just the smarter one and, unlike him, recognized a lost cause when she saw one. Not that he blamed her. He hadn't exactly given her reason to believe she could count on him to stick around when the shit hit the fan. Not after he'd hightailed it six hundred miles south the minute their marriage hit a brick wall the size of the Hoover Dam.

What the hell was he thinking? The cause of their

separation hadn't changed. What made him think for a second they'd ever reach a compromise? Sure, the sex was undeniably incredible, but that was hardly enough to warrant a lasting reconciliation. They held polar views. He wanted a family. Mikki didn't. End of marriage.

He muttered a curse and stood. Okay, so maybe what he really had was nothing more than a major hard-on for his wife. Mikki did have a way of digging under a man's skin in a big way. Get her into his bed and the hell out of his system—for good this time. Problem solved.

Except Mikki was not an easy woman to forget. After only two days she had him so tied up in knots with wanting her he couldn't think straight. He was confusing lust with longevity, and that wasn't enough of a reason to intentionally complicate his life by employing the ridiculous idea they stood a snowball's chance at a reconciliation.

Or did it?

"Aw, hell." There was nothing common or sensible about his feelings for Mikki. He didn't need to get laid. What he needed was a hard reality check.

"Or therapy," he muttered.

He forced himself to concentrate on the photographs he'd spread over the surface of massive rosewood desk he still considered his father's. He studied the pictures of nine-year-old Zoe Delaney and attempted to formulate a strong enough argument to sway the court to rule in his client's favor. Only, after the hours he'd spent reviewing reams of social service documentation, medical records and a handful of police incident reports, he faced better odds in convincing Mikki to give their marriage a shot at survival than he did of the court granting custody to his client, Zoe's biological mother, after she'd abandoned her kid for seven years.

It didn't help his case that the mother hadn't even bothered to contact her daughter until the public notices were published in the newspaper once the foster parents caring for Zoe had initiated adoption proceedings because the law required consent of the birth parents, provided they could be found. Zoe's biological father had been murdered in prison, but Nolan's client, Zoe's biological mother , who was currently married to a prominent San Francisco businessman, was petitioning the court not only to prevent the adoption, but to regain custody of her daughter.

Gathering the glossy evidence photos depicting injuries the child had suffered at the hands of her own father, Nolan paused. The hollow emptiness in the large, round blue eyes of the Delaney girl haunted him, but he couldn't drag his gaze away.

As he stared at a particularly disturbing Polaroid shot taken by an emergency room nurse, equal shares of anger and frustration nipped at him. He'd been practicing law in the family courts long enough to know minors were all too often hurt by the very adults supposed to protect them. In his line of work, he'd been privy to several unbelievable accounts, but until his review of Zoe Delaney's history, he'd been incapable of imagining the extent of deprivation this kid had suffered.

As a rule, he despised losing anything, especially a case. He diligently applied every legal maneuver at his disposal to collect more successes than failures. However unethical, he was powerless to prevent the clouding of his judgment. Mitigating circumstances be damned. If he were the judge hearing this case, he wouldn't grant the petitioner custody of a rag doll, let alone that of the daughter she'd abandoned, leaving her in the care of an abusive, sorry excuse for a father.

With a sound of disgust, he dropped the rest of the photos into the padded envelope, then returned them, along with the file, to the open briefcase resting on the elaborately carved, rosewood credenza. He needed a drink. One strong enough to wash the foul taste from his mouth.

He crossed the spacious, formal study of the Telegraph Hill residence he'd always hated to the liquor cabinet, where he snagged a crystal decanter from the sterling-silver serving tray. After pouring himself a generous portion of the contents into a matching crystal tumbler, he tossed it back as if he were pounding tequila shots with Tuck after a long, hot day on a construction site. Two decades' worth of old resentment began to instantly simmer in his gut, fueled by his old man's perfectly aged, twelve-year-old Scotch.

His hand tightened on the tumbler and he consciously loosened his grip before he shattered the glass. There'd been a time when he hadn't hated his father.

He'd even idolized the bastard, until he eventually discovered the truth—that Trenton Baylor had been nothing more than a coldhearted, self-serving SOB willing to sacrifice his family if it helped him advanced his political career.

For as long as Nolan could remember, his mother had suffered from severe depression. When he'd been little, he hadn't understood the extent of her illness, only that she'd lock herself in her room for days at a time, refusing to see him. Eventually she'd disappeared for weeks, sometimes months. Initially he turned to his father, instinctively, he supposed now, in an attempt to fill the void left by his missing mother. But with each of Clarice Baylor's absences, his old man had become more and more aloof, distancing himself not only from his emotionally unstable wife, but his own confused son.

Nolan had hated him for it. Renewed anger claimed him and he poured more Scotch into the tumbler, downing half in one swallow. The memories remained stubbornly fresh in his mind.

Long before he'd reached his teens, he'd discovered his mom's disappearances were spent as a patient in one of the best private psychiatric hospitals the Baylor money could buy. As he'd grown older, he'd understood his mother was mentally ill and had quickly learned to take advantage of her brief periods of lucidity. Those times never lasted more than a couple of weeks, and were never enough.

Disgusted by his own morose thoughts, Nolan threw

back the last of the booze, then set the empty tumbler on the tray before he left the study. His footsteps echoed in the cavernous corridor as he strode toward the sterile kitchen in search of sustenance.

He unearthed a covered casserole in the fridge, prepared by the housekeeper his assistant, Ozzie Parish, had hired and whom Nolan had only seen on a handful of occasions. God, how he despised the impersonal house, filled with ridiculously expensive antiques and designer furnishings, original works of art—and too many bad memories. He'd sell the damned place, but the house had been in the Baylor family for four generations and had miraculously survived the 1906 earthquake. Tradition and roots had become important to him in recent years and, as much as he disliked the cold sterility of the place, he couldn't bring himself to unload the property.

He considered giving a Tuck a shout, until he remembered his friend had been summoned to help out his oldest sister, Didi. If Nolan called, he knew from years of experience he'd be more than welcome. Just as he'd always been, he thought, ever since he and Tuck had become friends during their first year of junior high, after Nolan had gotten himself kicked out of another expensive boarding school.

His father had been under the mistaken belief that forcing his son to attend public school would serve as a fitting punishment. Out of spite, Nolan had become a model student. The joke had been on Trenton Baylor then, since the old man's political cronies had convinced him that a son excelling in the public school system could prove advantageous in the next election.

With his father's attention elsewhere and his mother's periods of hospitalization becoming lengthier with each subsequent readmission, there hadn't been anyone around to notice, or to care for that matter, when he began spending longer periods of time at the Schulz residence than at the house on Telegraph Hill.

At Tuck's, no one spoke in hushed tones, but shouted to be heard over the din of five siblings all fighting over the same bathroom. No servants hovered nearby to cater to the whims of the members of the household. In the Schulz home, every family member pitched in and pulled their own weight. He'd never told a soul, even his best friend, but he'd sworn he'd one day have a family life like Tuck's all his own.

Retrieving the casserole from the fridge, he slipped it inside the microwave to heat as the neatly printed instructions taped to the top of the dish instructed. He tilted the lid and caught a whiff of seafood. He wouldn't find so much as a single flake of tuna, he thought, struck by a craving for casserole made with homemade egg noodles he and Tuck would swipe from the cooling rack when they thought Tuck's mom, Sharon, wasn't looking. He'd give anything for a thick slice of her devil's food cake and a tall glass of ice-cold milk right now.

The thought of a genuine home-cooked meal nearly sent him on a search for the cordless phone, but the ringing of the doorbell stopped him. He pressed the keypad on the microwave to start cooking the casserole before heading for the door, expecting to find Tuck. Aside from the housekeeper, his friend was the only one who knew the security code necessary to gain entrance past the private security gate at street level.

He swung the door open. The greeting on his lips evaporated and his stomach bottomed out at the sight of Mikki, looking anxious and beautiful, standing on the brick porch. The lethally short, stop-sign-red dress outlining her voluptuous curves to perfection, sent a rush of fire through his veins and had his dick rock-hard. He skimmed his gaze down the length of her, past the flirty flounce of a hem that barely reached midthigh, to a pair of shiny black stilettos that added a few inches to her petite height and made her legs appear as if they went on forever.

Suddenly he was ravenous and his appetite had nothing whatsoever to do with food.

"Wow," he said once he found his voice. "That's some dress." Only a woman with Mikki's confidence could pull off such a bold look. The low scooped neckline left little to his imagination, which had already sped into overdrive.

"I have a date," she said saucily as she breezed past him in a cloud of red silk and familiar perfume. "Not that it's any of your business."

Disappointment slammed into him, followed by a razor-sharp slice of jealousy. She had a point, but that didn't mean he had to like the idea of another man drooling over *his* wife.

"Dressed like that?" He closed the door a little too hard. "Where are you meeting him? In the Tenderloin?" he asked, naming San Francisco's infamous red-light district.

She nailed him with her gaze. "What's it to you?"

He crossed his arms and frowned at her. "Maybe I don't like the thought of my wife going out with some other guy—" he intentionally stared at her cleavage despite the cost to his libido "—looking as if she charges by the hour."

Her brilliant blue eyes sizzled with fire, exciting the hell out of him. "*Ex*-wife," she reminded him.

She thrust a thick envelope at him before he managed a comeback. "Here," she said. "I did your homework for you. You have no excuse not to file that motion first thing Monday morning."

He took the heavy envelope, unable to resist sliding his fingers over hers in a feathery caress. She might be going out with someone else, but he planned to make damned sure all she thought about was him.

His touch had the desired effect. Her eyes rounded in surprise. The air surrounding them grew thick with tension. For as much as Mikki might protest otherwise, no way in hell was she immune to him.

Over a long time ago, my ass.

"Let me guess," he said, not bothering to open the envelope. "Applicable case law." More like the entire Westlaw database, based on the weight of the envelope.

"I gave you several points and authorities to support the court's validating our divorce. My declaration is in there, too. All you have to do is prep the motion and your declaration. You can even have your assistant do it."

"And since you were in the neighborhood, on your way to meet your date, you figured you'd just drop it by so I could get started right away, is that it?"

Her need for control obviously hadn't waned since he'd last seen her. Despite her diligent efforts to be rid of him, he doubted the system would make it that easy. In fact, he expected the judge to deny the motion and order them to file a new petition to dissolve their marriage. Which was fine by him since it'd buy him six months minimum to convince her they never should've separated in the first place. How he planned to do so, however, he'd play by ear.

"Exactly." Her hand trembled as she gave the shoulder strap of her purse a minor adjustment. "Now, if you'll excuse me."

Mikki? Nervous? He eyed her suspiciously, wondering what had really prompted her visit tonight. Knowing her as well as he did, he supposed there was only one foolproof way to get to the truth. Piss her off. Royally.

She took a tentative step toward the door. "Have your assistant call my office once the date and time are set."

He moved to stand in front of her, blocking to path. "What's the rush? You just got here."

"I, uh…"

He trailed his hand lightly down her arm and took

hold of her wrist. Her pulse fluttered wildly beneath his touch.

She briefly frowned, then quickly recovered, offering up a manufactured smile. "I have a date. Remember?"

She was so full of it, and they both knew it. "Sure you do," he said, intentionally baiting her.

She looked up at him, a deadly combination of longing and irritation evident in her gaze. "Excuse me?"

The irritation didn't faze him. The longing gave him hope, and a clue. Oh, yeah, she had a date all right—with destiny.

MIKKI COULDN'T BREATHE. Being so close to Nolan did that to her. She really shouldn't let him get to her. For crying out loud, she'd lived with the man, had slept beside him in the same bed, yet she'd quickly come to the disturbing conclusion that when it came to Nolan Baylor, any hope of her behaving rationally seemed impossible.

Within range of all that blatant male sex appeal, her willpower failed. But she hated loose ends and taking charge of her life before it spun too far out of control didn't include leaving anything to chance, especially the annoying matter of her divorce from Nolan.

"Are you going to tell me the real reason why you came all the way over here tonight? Or are you going to make me guess?"

Her pulse leaped at the all-too-knowing smile lifting one corner of his mouth, zapping her flimsy facade of confidence. "Because I know you, Nolan."

Because I haven't been able to stop fantasizing about making love to you again.

"Do you?" he asked, his voice smooth.

Did she ever. On all counts. It didn't help her cause that he was so damned unforgettable, either.

"I know you'd be content to let this mess go unresolved."

A single dark eyebrow zinged upward. "What's the hurry? Marriage cramping your style?"

She worked hard to summon an icy glare, but from the way his smile deepened, she had a feeling she'd lost her chill factor.

"I have a life, you know," she said. "I'd like to get on with it."

He shrugged carelessly. "So you petition the court."

She would, if she thought for a minute the court would grant the motion without her having to explain why she'd been unable to travel to Mexico personally. She let out a sigh. "Coming from you, it'll carry more weight. My attorney was disbarred, remember? As far as the courts are concerned, I never even made an appearance. If you petition the court, then as respondent, I would only have to file a reply brief to make an appearance. Do it, Nolan. I want this over and done with for good."

He tossed the envelope onto a nearby chest. "Nice try, babe, but you know the law as well as I do. There isn't a judge in the state that will validate our divorce." He turned and took off down the corridor.

Unwilling to concede defeat, she hurried after him, the click of her four-inch heels echoing loudly over the imported marble tiles. Consciously she slowed her steps. Electing to wear the ridiculous skyscraper heels hadn't been her wisest choice, but she hadn't expected to literally have to chase after Nolan.

She followed him into the kitchen, ten times the size of her small cramped one. The daring red dress hadn't been such a hot idea, either, but she'd been striving to project an illusion of confidence. She felt guilty for lying about having a date, but she'd suddenly felt ridiculous and way too obvious in a getup that all but guaranteed he'd be driven to his knees. Still, the hungry look in his eyes when he'd answered the door had lessened her insecurity somewhat.

She hadn't expected her plan to backfire on her, though. Another fine mess she'd made.

"You're wrong," she blurted, sounding more like a sulky child than an accomplished lawyer.

"I doubt it," he countered dismissively.

Her temper instantly flared. The little red beaded bag she'd been carrying landed on the stainless center island with a loud thwack. "Hardly. In *Peterson* the appellate court upheld the lower court's ruling that a Mexican divorce was valid even though the attorney for the petitioner left Juarez, Mexico, prior to the requisite forty-eight-hour period," she argued vehemently.

"Sure," he agreed, and opened the microwave. "But counsel representing the petitioner had been legally licensed by the state to practice law. Plus, there were extenuating circumstances preventing him from staying in Mexico."

He pulled out a casserole dish and set it on the island, then gave her a condescending smile that spiked her blood pressure despite her admiration for his innate ability to argue case law.

"And your attorney was already disbarred when he appeared on your behalf," he added.

As if she needed the reminder. "What about *Jacobs*? The court denied the respondent's motion to have their divorce declared invalid." Bracing her hands on the edge of the island, she leaned forward and gave him a level stare, daring him to counter that argument.

He had the gall to smile at her. Slowly he circled the island to move in behind her. Distance was key to her survival. She knew it, yet her body refused to budge. The feel of him, his heat enveloping her, his arms surrounding her, were too potent for her to resist.

"Won't fly," he whispered.

His warm breath fanned her ear and she tipped her head to the side. His fly rubbed against her bottom. Tension coiled tightly inside her and she closed her eyes as his hands skimmed past her hips to glide sinuously down to her thighs. Oh, how she missed this, missed him.

"Why not?" Without thinking, she rocked her hips against him. She no longer knew if she was asking for clarification on the point of law they were debating or for something she had no business entertaining.

The man was twice as dangerous to her as an open bottle of booze, and ten times more intoxicating. Like the addict she was, she greedily welcomed the fix he offered.

"Because," he said casually, as if his teasing kisses on the tender spot below her ear weren't driving her to distraction. "The respondent wanted the divorce invalidated to claim community property rights to a winning lottery ticket. A ticket that her husband had purchased after he'd fulfilled the forty-eight-hour waiting period."

The tips of his fingers grazed the backs of her legs. Her lipstick-red lace thong rasped enticingly against her swollen sex, heightening her desire. He urged her to widen her stance. She wouldn't dream of refusing and shifted her feet slightly apart.

"Ah," he murmured encouragingly against her throat. "And Mrs. Jacobs was already in Mexico at the time her husband bought the lottery ticket, indicating intent to fulfill the requirements prescribed by the law."

He caught her earlobe between his teeth and bit down gently. Her senses came alive when he slipped his hand beneath the hem of her dress to caress her bottom, kneading the flesh with his large, warm hands. The lace rubbed against her clit, creating such a wickedly erotic sensation, her breath quickened in anticipation of a more intimate exploration. A low moan erupted from inside her and she rocked her hips back, pressing herself firmly against his very impressive erection. A shudder passed over her.

"Okay, we could have a problem here." Whether she meant her legal argument or the insistent tug of desire making her wet and impossibly swollen and aching for his touch, she wasn't sure.

"It doesn't have to be." His voice grew huskier, deeper.

The alternating biting kisses and teasing sweeps of his tongue on the exposed nape of her neck added to her confusion. "I can't jump through all those hoops again," she said before another moan escaped. Regardless of which conversation they were having, her response applied to both the law and the monumental mistake there were about to make.

He leaned over her and dragged his hands down her hips, pushing aside the flimsy barrier of lace. "Then don't."

If only it were that straightforward. The fact that she'd attended an AA meeting this afternoon should be more than enough to remind her that their relationship could never be classified as simple. Right now, she didn't care about simple. She only cared about the pleasure Nolan would give her.

Her back arched and she gripped the table for support as he opened her slick folds, exposing her. With the expertise of a man who knew exactly how to please his wife, he used the pad of his thumb to apply the perfect degree of pressure as he stroked her throbbing sex.

She immediately flew over the edge. Delightful spasms rumbled through her in delicious waves. She cried out from the unexpected rush of exquisite sensation and rode high on the crest until the spectacular vibrations coursing through her ebbed.

She lay bent over the stainless-steel island, struggling to catch her breath, wondering what the hell she was supposed to do now. Of all the stupid, asinine stunts she could've pulled, this one deserved a place in the Idiots Hall of Shame.

Suddenly uncomfortable, she attempted to wiggle free. Nolan pulled her to him and gently turned her to face him. Her heart lurched at the tenderness in his eyes. She couldn't do this. Not again. God, when would she ever learn to stay away from him?

He cupped her face in his hands and brushed his lips lightly over hers. "Was being married to me really that difficult?"

She briefly closed her eyes against the sharp pain in her chest. "No, Nolan, it wasn't," she said, slipping out of his embrace. "It was divorcing you that nearly killed me."

6

"THAT'S THE PROBLEM with giving in to a moment of passion," Rory said to Lauren. "You always have to deal with the morning after. It's a cosmic rule."

Mikki coughed, nearly choking on the forkful of *tourtière* she'd just shoveled into her mouth. She made a grab for her double shot caramel latte and took a large gulp, scalding her tongue. If there was an ounce of truth to what Rory just said, Mikki feared she would be facing the equivalent of a cosmic catastrophe.

Wham, bam, thank you, sir!

With the way her luck had turned, she just knew that mind-blowing orgasm would eventually come back to haunt her. At least she'd gone straight home and hadn't tempted fate by heading for the first watering hole she could find. Surely that counted for something.

She hoped.

An odd glint entered her mom's too wise gaze as she filled a delicate china teapot with boiling water from the kettle. "Tea?" Emma Constable offered innocently, sending Mikki's suspicions soaring.

She wrinkled her nose at the heavy aroma of smoked

jasmine filling the air. "No, thanks," she told her mom. "I'm still working on my latte."

"So you guys think I should back away?" Lauren asked, referring to the intimate encounter she'd had at the key party Friday night. Lauren didn't normally chase after men, but the disappointment in her eyes made it apparent she had a thing for the guy who'd unlocked her possibilities, and then some, at the party.

For once in her life Mikki possessed enough wisdom to keep her mouth firmly closed. On the subject of men, she was clearly unqualified to offer advice. Unfortunately her silence spoke louder than any commentary she might have offered based on the expectant expressions on the faces of the women seated at the large, heavy oak table in the cozy kitchen.

She took another sip of her latte, her gaze darting to each of the occupants. Rory and Emma both stared at her. Lauren appeared mildly confused by the sudden tension, shrugged and toyed with her food.

"What?" Mikki let out an impatient huff of breath. "Quit looking at me like that."

Lauren paused, fork poised in midair. "Uh-oh, what'd I miss?"

Hoping to deflect all that attention aimed in her direction, Mikki frowned. "If you're going to disappear off the radar, Lauren, expect to miss a few minidramas."

Her sister laughed, taking no offense. "Oh, look who's talking. I called you last night around ten o'clock, and all I got was voice mail."

Mikki shrugged. "I could've been asleep, you know," she muttered.

"But you weren't." Rory sounded too much like their mother for Mikki's piece of mind. Somehow Rory had managed to cultivate that same innate sixth sense when it came to her family as Emma, which had always made it impossible for any of them to pull the tie-dye over their mom's eyes. "At least not in your own bed," she added.

Mikki refused to look at her sister. "I wasn't in Nolan's bed, either, if that's what you're implying." Well, she wasn't. Not technically, anyway.

"So where *did* you and Nolan have sex?" Lauren's voice brimmed with laughter.

Mikki let out a defeated sigh and slumped against the hard rails of the oak chair. "Does the concept of privacy mean anything in this house?"

Lauren's grinned widened. "Not especially."

"Not that I can remember," Rory added.

Emma absently stirred her tea, spooning a few stray tea leaves from her cup. "The wheel never stops turning." She examined the tea leaves on her spoon through a pair of bifocals. "What goes around comes around, Mikki," she warned over the rim of her glasses. "Surely you've realized that by now."

Mikki leaned forward and propped her elbows on the table. She dropped her chin into the palm of her hand and let out a weighty sigh. "That's what has me worried."

Lauren nudged Rory with her elbow. "She *did* have sex with him. I knew it."

"Well…" Mikki hedged. "Sort of."

Three pairs of eyebrows winged skyward simultaneously.

"Oh, hell, I don't know what happened," she blurted, straightening. "Or even *how,* for that matter. One minute we were arguing case law and the next thing I know, I'm having an incredible orgasm."

"Incredible or really incredible?" Lauren asked.

Mikki let out another sigh. "Really, *really* incredible."

"Does this means the divorce is off?" Rory asked, sounding concerned.

"Hardly," Mikki said. "Last night doesn't change a thing. Nolan and I were over ages ago."

"Perhaps," Emma said thoughtfully. "But perhaps not."

Perfect. Just what she *didn't* want to hear. "Can the mystic wisdom, Mom," Mikki warned. "I don't care how many white-speckled owls land on the roof three-point-two seconds after sunrise, or even if the planets aligned themselves with Venus at the precise moment I came, Nolan and I are *not* meant to be together. We'd kill each other within a week."

As usual, Emma remained the epitome of serenity. "The universe has its own a unique way of putting things to rights in the end."

"It did when we split up," Mikki argued.

Rory forked a tomato from her salad and laughed. "If it ain't broke…"

"Finally," Mikki said with an elaborate hand gesture. "We have the voice of reason."

Emma indulged in a second helping of *tourtière*. Mikki didn't miss Rory's covetous glance, similar to the way she'd been looking at Tucker the night of the key party. Mikki might not recall much of the evening, but she had a distinct memory of her sister and Tuck doing more than dancing at Clementine's.

"Then how do you explain your divorce being invalid?" Emma challenged, forcing Mikki's attention back to her own problems.

Lauren snickered. "Karma."

Mikki ignored that comment. "Rotten luck," she told her mom. "And a temporary inconvenience. One that will hopefully be rectified by the end of the week. Nolan is filing a motion with enough legal precedent even the Pope would be convinced our divorce should be recognized. I'll be permanently single by next weekend."

At least she'd better be single, she thought, though she couldn't shake her worries over his lack of enthusiasm to officially end their marriage. Surely after all this time he didn't imagine he still loved her.

Could he?

It didn't matter. When two people were as wrong for each other as they were, divorce was the only answer.

"A rubber stamp on a piece of paper isn't going to change the way you and Nolan feel about each other," Emma said sagely. "If you're meant to be together, you will be."

Lauren set her fork on the edge of her plate. "Maybe Mom has a point," she said, frowning. "How does that saying go? Everything happens for a reason?"

"Good point," Emma confirmed. She spread a slab of salt-free butter over one of the warmed rolls from Rory's shop. "You can't mess with fate."

"Fate? Now there's a load of crap I'm won't be buying," Mikki argued fiercely. "What possible reason could exist for this kind of disruption in my life?"

Rory propped her arms on the table and laced her fingers together. "Unfinished business."

"Unresolved emotions." Lauren shot Mikki a meaningful glance. "Lots of them."

Her sisters were not helping. Mikki sounded off with an indignant huff, then stood to begin clearing the table. "It's over," she reminded them again, "and has been for a long time."

"Really?" Emma handed her a blue-and-yellow covered dish she'd made herself in pottery class. "Then why did you drive up to Telegraph Hill to see him last night?"

"To give him the relevant case law I'd researched," Mikki said defensively.

Emma's tolerant, albeit disbelieving, expression almost had her fessing up.

Following the AA meeting and an early dinner with her sponsor, she'd been filled with renewed determination to tie up the loose ends of her marriage. She'd gone to the law library to conduct research and by the time she'd finished, she'd been too keyed up to sleep.

Or so she'd tried to tell herself. The truth wasn't quite so straightforward, and she did understand her going to Nolan's had been nothing more than the trading of one vice for another. Instead of waking up with a hangover, she'd suffered with a truckload of recrimination instead…and a craving twice as addictive as any bottle of eighty proof.

Emma continued to look at her skeptically. Considering the paper-thin excuse she'd just tried to feed her, Mikki expected no less.

"You couldn't e-mail it to him?" Emma asked her.

Mikki's frown returned. "No," she answered, "I couldn't. I wanted…"

Nolan.

God, she was so screwed. No twelve-step program existed to help her resist the intoxicating pull of desire that continually drew her to him. There were no sponsors to call when the need for him became too overwhelming. When it came to Nolan, there was no one to save her from her own self-destructive behavior.

She walked to the sink and set the dishes in the pan of soapy water and gazed through the opening in her mom's funky chicken-and-rooster café curtains to the deck. Countless wind chimes fluttered and twirled on the breeze amid an array of hanging pots filled with a variety of flowers. Large plastic and wooden planters filled with organic vegetables in early growing stages fought for floor space on the wooden deck interspersed among redwood Adirondack chairs.

"I wanted Nolan," she admitted. She turned to face them. "I went to his place for sex. Satisfied."

Emma smiled. "I'm sure you were," she quipped.

"What's the big deal, anyway? The guy's a great

lay. What happened last night changes nothing. Incredible multiple orgasms won't change the fact that Nolan and I will always be wrong for each other."

"So *you* say," Emma said, then rose and walked to where Mikki stood by the sink. Slipping her arm across Mikki's shoulders, she gave her a comforting hug. "But what does Nolan say?"

"I don't know, Mom. We can't be in the same room for more than five minutes without going for the jugular."

"That's not all they go for," Lauren teased.

Emma smoothed a lock of dark hair from Mikki's face. "When the secrets are all told," she said, "the petals all unfold."

Emma turned and absently sidestepped the hideous hanging macramé sculpture suspended from the twelve-foot beam separating the kitchen and living room. Mikki waited until Emma left the kitchen, then looked at her sisters and lifted her hands in a helpless gesture. "Any clue what that's supposed to mean?"

Lauren shook her head. "Something Jerry probably told her once," she said, referring to their mother's long-ago friendship with the late Jerry Garcia.

"More than likely," Rory agreed. A slow grin crossed her face when she looked up at Mikki. "Whatever it means, I have a feeling you probably wouldn't like the translation."

"No doubt," Mikki mumbled, dipping her hands into the soapy water. As mystified as she was by her mom's colorful past, Mikki couldn't deny the effectiveness of

Emma's unique talent for making her think about things she'd rather not face—like the truth.

NOLAN'S CONCENTRATION was shot. If he didn't get his head in the game of eight ball, he'd be shelling out three more twenties to Tucker. Only a fool went double or nothing on a losing streak, but he'd fallen for Tuck's taunt like a desperate gambler two minutes before the closing bell of the last race at Hollywood Park.

Nolan took aim, sent the cue ball zinging across the green-felt pool table right into the corner pocket, missing the striped purple ball he'd been aiming for by a good three inches or more.

Tuck didn't bother to hide his smirk. "I don't know what Mikki did to you last night, buddy, but I'm not about to complain." He rounded the table, looking for his next shot. "It must have been some number, huh?"

Nolan moved away from the pool table to give Tuck room. "That obvious?"

Tuck responded with more laughter. "Must be the challenge," he said, leaning down to line up his shot. The cue ball rolled smoothly over the table to nick the edge of the solid orange ball, sending it cleanly into the side pocket. "I think you're just a glutton for punishment. Some guys get off on that, you know."

Nolan reached for the half-empty bottle of beer sitting on the nearby table in the billiard room of the house on Telegraph Hill. He took a long pull and considered Tuck's remark. Was his obsession with Mikki because he loved her or strictly about the challenge she presented?

He wasn't sure he liked the answer. Fiercely competitive, he did hate losing and his record in the courtroom stood as testament to his determination to collect more wins than losses. He'd only run from one challenge in his life: his marriage to Mikki. So did that mean his wanting her now stemmed from the desire to correct a wrong or some twisted need to salve his battered ego where she was concerned?

Maybe the answer was just a simple case of lust but, then, nothing about his marriage to Mikki had ever qualified as uncomplicated. No reason to think that aspect of their relationship had changed in their time apart.

Tuck lined up another shot. "Maybe you should think about finding a woman who isn't so hard to handle," he said, looking over his shoulder at Nolan.

"Like Rory?" Nolan returned with a calculated grin.

Tuck missed his shot, his cue stick skimming the surface of the white ball. "We're just friends," he said in a firm tone.

"You could do worse," Nolan reminded him. "And have." He recalled a particularly clingy blonde Tuck had had difficulty shaking loose. "So when are you taking Rory to Mendocino for the weekend?"

"I'm not *taking* her to Mendocino." Tuck straightened and cast an impatient glance Nolan's way. "We won a prize at the party, that's it. We'll probably even take separate cars."

"But not separate beds."

Tuck flipped him the bird, but Nolan only chuckled.

As if he should talk. Courtesy of his wife, he'd been plagued with a constant ache that showed no signs of relenting anytime soon.

No one to blame but yourself, pal.

He couldn't argue with that logic, even if it was too little, too late. But then, he hadn't expected Mikki to take off the way she had, either, obliterating any possibility of the night of lovemaking he'd been so sure they'd be enjoying. He'd been unable to get her out of his mind since, not that she was ever all that far from his thoughts in the first place.

It was divorcing you that nearly killed me.

Her parting comment continued to nag him as it had most of the night and into the following day. He'd made it clear to her he hadn't wanted the divorce, not only yesterday before he'd left her apartment, but even back when she'd kept pressuring him to fly down to Mexico and "just get it the hell over with." If she hadn't wanted the divorce, why had she kept insisting otherwise?

He bent low to line up his aim on the striped purple ball near the side pocket, took his shot and missed. Snagging his beer in frustration, he lifted the bottle to take another long pull, then paused. "Did you talk to Mikki much after I moved to L.A.?" he asked suddenly.

"I called her a few times to see how she was doing," Tuck said. "You know, just to remind her if she needed anything, any repairs around the apartment, whatever, that she knew where to find me."

"Did she take you up on your offer?"

Tuck gave him a get-real look. "You know Mikki," he said. "Too damned independent for her own good most of the time."

"So you never saw her, then?"

Tuck stood on the opposite side of the table, with the pool stick in his hands, the rubber tip planted on the floor between his feet. "What do you mean?" he asked cautiously.

"Did you see her around much?" Nolan pressed. "Run into her?"

"Here or there," Tuck answered. "Saw her at the Lighthouse Grill down on the marina a couple of times. Why?"

"How'd she seem to you?"

His friend shrugged, then walked the length of the pool table, keeping his gaze on the colorful balls still in play. "I dunno," he said. "It's been a couple years."

"But you remember seeing her at the Lighthouse Grill." He didn't bother to keep the accusation out of his voice, certain Tuck was keeping something from him.

"Like I said, it's been a couple years."

"But not long enough for you to forget where you saw her," Nolan said. "That's a pretty specific detail."

"Hey." Tuck shot him an exasperated look. "What gives? Why the cross-examination?"

"Cut the bullshit, Tuck," he warned his friend. "What aren't you telling me?"

Tuck let out a rough sigh and lay his cue stick across the pool table. "What difference does it make?" Tuck fired back at him. He crossed his arms and gave Nolan a hard stare. "You'd been in L.A. for a few months by then, the marriage was over and you'd both moved on. Let it go."

"I don't give a damn if she was with some other guy." His lips were moving and he was definitely lying, giving credence to the old lawyer joke. Just the thought of Mikki with another man had that ugly, green-eyed monster charging out of its hiding place. "I'm curious is all," he said, tempering his voice. "Something she said to me last night just made me wonder."

It was divorcing you that nearly killed me.

"She wasn't with any guy," Tuck told him. "The first time I ran into her, she was with a group of women."

"And the next?"

"She was alone, and I bought her a drink. Anyone with big enough balls to approach her, she'd cut to ribbons with that sharp tongue of hers." A wry grin tugged Tuck's mouth. "You know what she's like."

Did he ever. He'd been on the receiving end of that Irish-Sicilian temper more times than he cared to recall. But damn, he loved her passion, and Mikki had an abundance of the stuff.

The first time he'd spoken to her had been on a rainy Friday afternoon at the law library. They had had a Torts class together, and his interest had been sparked by all that wild, black-as-midnight hair, her bombshell curves and the biggest, bluest eyes he'd ever seen. But it had been her knowledge of the law, her vibrancy when she debated court decisions in class, and the enthusiasm with which

she expressed her opinions that had initially capti-
vated him.

Although the library had been fairly empty of stu-
dents, he'd approached her to ask if the seat across
from her was available. She'd shot him down so quickly
he hadn't even seen the lash of that razor-sharp tongue
coming. She'd looked him up and down and had replied
with an abrupt yes, it was, then added that hers would
be, too, if he didn't get lost.

Her dismissal had only intrigued him more. It'd
taken him weeks to wear her down, but he'd been determined to win her over so he'd continued to pester her
until she'd eventually given in and gone out with him.
Not long afterward, they'd moved in together. Their
final year of law school, they'd run off to Las Vegas to
get married. Oh sure, they'd argued plenty during their
marriage, mainly just differences of opinion, which he
supposed was to be expected considering her passion-
ate nature, but still they'd been happy.

He'd wanted to start a family right away, but she'd
been less than enthusiastic and he'd let her convince him
they should wait until they both had steady jobs. Since
he'd refused any financial assistance beyond tuition
from his father, he'd conceded Mikki had made a valid
point.

Only employment hadn't been enough for him, and
although Mikki had begun to accuse him of not taking
life too seriously because she took life seriously enough
for both of them, he'd broached the subject of family a
few months later. She'd said she wasn't ready to tackle

motherhood while attempting to launch her career. Disappointed in her reluctance, he'd put his dreams temporarily on hold, telling himself they had plenty of years ahead of them.

Always one to thrive under a challenge, he'd became bored and restless. In need of a more fulfilling position than what clerking for an appellate court judge provided, and without first consulting Mikki, he'd applied for a position with a large, prestigious firm based in Los Angeles and had been hired. Rather than working out of the San Francisco office, the job required him to relocate to Southern California. He'd accepted, figuring with the salary he'd be pulling in, he'd finally obliterate Mikki's argument of waiting to start a family until they were more financially secure. For a few short hours, he'd mistakenly believed the future was his to own.

He couldn't have been more wrong.

When he'd told her about the job, she'd been supportive and enthusiastic, until he'd informed her of the plans he had for their future. She'd been livid, vehemently refusing to leave San Francisco, her job and her family. They'd argued for hours, about his taking the offer without consulting her, his refusal to reconcile with his father and her staunch refusal to move to L.A., and how she kept putting off their starting a family. He remembered saying something particularly nasty about her being a hypocrite on the issues of family, and that's when she'd blindsided him with the truth—she never had any intention of having a child. Ever.

As hard as he'd tried, he hadn't been able to get a straight answer out of her. The more he'd pushed, the harder she'd pushed back. He didn't get it. She worked as a child advocate, a court appointed Guardian ad Litem representing the rights of minors. He'd occasionally watched her in court, saw her interact with the young clients she represented, and it had always been blatantly obvious to him when it came to dealing with kids, Mikki was magic.

But she'd refused to budge on the issue, and for the first time in his life, he'd lost the desire to go after what he'd wanted. Just like his old man, he thought now. When life veered from the course, distance once again was the Baylor cure.

He looked over at Tuck and forced a grin. "She can be a major pain the ass," he said, lightening his tone in an effort to shake off the dark memories.

"Especially when she's had a few too many." Tuck gave an exaggerated shudder. "Viperous, man. Mikki's one hell of a woman, but I don't get the attraction. There are more fish in the sea, buddy."

But they aren't Mikki.

Only Mikki made him feel as if his heart would burst from his chest because it was filled to capacity with emotion. Only she had the power to excite him with one look from her big blue eyes, whether in anger, happiness and especially in bed. No matter how often he asked himself the same question, the answer made perfect sense to him. Not only was his wife a challenge and the woman he'd never stopped loving, she was exciting, vivacious and so full of passion he knew without a doubt that life with Mikki would never be cold and sterile but would be filled with warmth and noise and a whole lotta love.

7

"MOTION DENIED."

Mikki's stomach bottomed out.

Denied? No. That couldn't be right. The judge hadn't even allowed them oral argument in support of the motion Nolan had filed on their behalf. This couldn't be happening. Denied?

"But, Your Honor, we haven't yet—"

"Save it, counselor." Judge Eckerd glared at her from the bench, as if daring her to defy him in open court. "You want a divorce, file a petition like everybody else. My ruling stands." He dismissed her by shifting his attention to the middle-aged clerk to his left. "Next case."

Eckerd was famous for slapping outspoken attorneys with contempt fines and she couldn't afford another one of his outrageous sums because she didn't have sense enough to back down from a fight. Mustering every ounce of self-control at her disposal, she kept quiet and silently seethed.

She glanced in Nolan's direction, willing him to object or to say something—*anything*—to help. But he just sat there with what she could've sworn was a satisfied smirk on his handsome face. She'd had a bad feeling today's hearing wouldn't go well. Despite her disappointment, Eckerd's ruling hardly surprised her, regardless of how unfair she viewed his decision. When Nolan's assistant had called her office Tuesday to inform her that the hearing was scheduled for Friday morning, she'd been elated—until she'd learned they would be appearing before Judge Reginald Eckerd. The former prosecutor was fanatically rigid, and whenever she'd appeared before him, never had she known him to stray so much as a fraction from the exact letter of the law.

She shoved her notes and copy of the motion into her briefcase and snapped the lid closed. Dammit, she should've known he wouldn't grant their motion, but she'd stupidly hoped otherwise. The legal argument in favor of upholding the divorce had been a strong one, too, but according to Eckerd, with no extenuating circumstances cited to indicate she'd been prevented from making the requisite forty-eight-hour appearance herself, he would not validate a technically corrupt divorce.

Locked up in court-ordered rehab was about as extenuating as a circumstance could get, but she wasn't about to reveal that dirty little secret. Her addiction was her business and only a select few knew of the twenty-eight days of hell she'd spent getting clean and sober. And she planned to keep it that way.

Fuming, she snagged her briefcase from the table and, without a word, left the courtroom. Fine. She'd file for divorce like everyone else. The sooner the better, too. In six months, all this would all be behind her.

Pushing through the heavy oak door, she stepped into the marbled corridor of the downtown courthouse and slumped against the nearest wall. Six months of being married to Nolan? *Why? Why?*

She needed air. Better yet, a drink to help choke down the bitter disappointment lodged in her throat.

She pulled in several deep breaths, striving for a calm she doubted she'd ever feel again. Okay, so she'd suffered a major setback. *Put it into perspective and get a grip.* If she didn't, she'd crumble and give in to the knifelike need for a drink. Six days of sobriety and as many AA meetings to help her stay sober were too valuable to allow Eckerd's ruling to push her off the wagon just when she was beginning to feel as if she'd found her footing again. Yes, she was upset. No, her plans hadn't gone the way she'd hoped. But swilling down a fifth of bourbon wasn't the solution.

She would stay clean. She had to, even if the disappointment would be a whole lot easier to handle after a shot or two.

What difference did six more months make, anyway? She hadn't seen or heard from Nolan since she'd shown up at his place, so it wasn't as if she had to worry about running into him all the time. Thinking about him, aching for his touch, well, that was another matter altogether, but she'd manage. With the exception of a couple of necessary court appearances for the divorce proceeding, she'd probably never see him again. No big deal. Right?

"Right," she murmured, but didn't sound all that convincing.

Feeling slightly more in control, she walked down the corridor toward the bank of elevators in the third-floor lobby. She was due to meet Maureen Baxter for lunch at the Sea Breeze Café in less than an hour to discuss several cases scheduled for hearings the following week. Tonight Mikki would begin on the petition for dissolution of marriage, and would have the process started no later than next Monday. By Thanksgiving, Nolan would be out of her life—for good this time.

The doors to the elevator slid closed before she reached them. Her frustration level climbed several degrees and she jammed her index finger repeatedly on the down button. Her freshly manicured nail snapped. "Damn. Damn. Damn."

"Mikki, wait up!"

"Go away," she warned. She kept her eyes on the snail's progress of the trio of elevators, praying for one to arrive pronto.

Each one stopped in succession—on other floors.

"We should talk."

Nolan's citrus-scented aftershave teased her senses. Heavens, but the man smelled good.

"You should stay the hell away from me," she said. "If you value your life, that is."

As usual, he ignored her and moved closer. His arm brushed her shoulder, sending an enticing shiver dancing down her spine. Her breasts tingled and she shifted uncomfortably in her three-inch heels.

A crush of people began to fill the lobby area. She knew a few of the attorneys and nodded an absent greeting in their direction. A court reporter she recognized smiled at her. She tried to be nice and return the smile, but the curve of her lips felt more like a grimace of pain.

"I warned you filing a motion would be a waste of time," he said in a smug tone.

Anger instantly revived, she whirled around to face him. "You chose Judge Eckerd, didn't you?" she accused, not caring that they were performing in front of an audience. "You knew that by-the-book son of a bitch would never grant the motion, so you had the motion put on his calendar intentionally."

The infuriating man had the nerve to actually smile at her. Smile? He obviously had a death wish.

"You don't seriously believe that, do you?"

With every last breath in my body.

She made a hissing sound between her teeth. "Go away, Nolan. Just go away." She spun back toward the bank of closed elevator doors, impatiently tapping her foot. "Get out of my life and stay out." She pressed the down button again. No elevator car arrived to provide a means of escape. "You did it before. Do it again. Please."

"Mikki, listen—"

"No!" She fired the word at him, not caring that her voice rose several decibels. She ignored the uncomfortable shifting of the people surrounding them and concentrated on Nolan. "You listen, and listen good. I do *not* want to stay married to you. Got it?"

He clamped his hand around her upper arm. "Excuse us," he said to the cluster of curious onlookers, steering her away from the lobby.

"Let go of me," she snarled. Naturally, he ignored that demand, too.

She didn't care to hear a word of whatever line of bullshit he was determined to feed her. She didn't want to be anywhere near him. Why couldn't he understand, or respect, that? He was her greatest weakness and she didn't possess enough strength to battle two addictions simultaneously.

"Don't say you weren't warned." She pulled her free arm back, twisted around and whacked his backside with her briefcase.

He tightened his hold, stopped and looked down at her. His luscious dark eyes filled with an electrifying combination of desire and amusement. "Don't think I won't throw your sweet little ass over my shoulder and carry you out of here if I have to, Mikki," he warned, his voice low and way too intoxicating for a Nolan-junkie like her to withstand. "Your choice."

Her temper soared. "Just try it," she dared him, narrowing her eyes.

He chuckled, then had the audacity to plant a quick hard kiss on her lips. He hauled her into the stairwell before she recovered from the rush of arousal caused by the pressure of his lips against hers. The thick, ivory metal door closed with a heavy clang and he pushed her up against the wall. His briefcase hit the landing a heartbeat after his mouth clamped firmly over hers in a hot, openmouthed kiss that stole her breath and had her body humming with acute awareness.

Her own mahogany-leather briefcase slipped from her fingers, landing with a heavy thud at their feet. Winding her arms around his neck, she aligned her body with his and deepened the kiss.

There was nothing gentle or tender about the way he kissed her, and that suited her just fine. She responded with equal hunger, raking her fingers through his hair to make certain he knew without a doubt she'd settle for nothing less than complete satisfaction to the demands of her body.

He set her on fire.

Thank heavens some things never changed.

His hands held her bottom so tight, she felt the bite of his fingers through the lightweight fabric of her scarlet-red skirt. She didn't much care if he left bruises so long as he continued kissing her as if he'd never stop.

His knee nudged hers and she shifted her stance to straddle his thigh. The snug fit of her skirt prevented her from feeling the pressure of his expensively clad leg against her throbbing and swollen clit. She moaned in frustration and he hiked her skirt up past her hips. Cool air brushed against her heated skin, from the tops of her stockings to her red satin thong. She pressed herself against him. White-hot need exploded inside her.

She pulled her arms from around his neck and fumbled frantically with the buttons of his white dress shirt, opening the placket enough so she could slip her hands beneath the fabric to smooth them over his rib cage. An earthy moan bubbled up from inside her the instant her fingertips came into contact with the warm texture of his skin. Five minutes ago she'd wanted to strangle him, and she still did, but not until she'd made love to him first.

His hands found her exposed backside, his fingers smoothing over the curves, driving her even more insane with need. Withdrawing her hand from his shirt, she trailed her fingers down to his fly where she cupped her hand over the length of his erection. Slowly she stroked him, causing his hips to buck against her hand. He emitted a deep, low growl of pleasure.

The tension building fast inside her climbed impossibly higher. Moisture pooled between her legs and she rocked harder against his thigh. The back of her throat tingled as she suckled his tongue. She imagined the long, hot length of his cock in her mouth and nearly came.

Her muddled senses registered the closing slam of a door somewhere above her. Footfalls on metal steps followed, along with the distinct sound of voices and laughter. She knew they had to stop, but she lacked the will, even if it meant being discovered.

Nolan obviously had more sense. He ended the kiss and she stared up at him in confusion. Wrapping his fingers around her wrist, he gently pulled her hand away. His eyes were filled with a reluctance that tugged hard on her heart.

No, not her heart, she reminded herself. Never her heart. She wouldn't allow it.

He carefully smoothed her skirt back into place. The cocky, self-assured half grin curving his mouth had her common sense flooding back to her in a rush.

Her hands trembled as she made an attempt to adjust her skirt and matching jacket. The thin straps of her black silk camisole had slid down her arms and were digging into her biceps, but she didn't care. All she wanted now was to escape that knowing grin on her husband's face, the one that said he knew she'd been close to the edge and that it hadn't mattered they were in the stairwell of the courthouse. They'd been on the brink, and nothing else had mattered to her except sexual gratification. If that realization alone couldn't qualify as a reminder of the dangers Nolan presented, then nothing ever would.

"Nothing's changed," she said in a hushed whisper. "I still want a divorce."

His grin only widened. "That makes one of us."

She looked frantically for her briefcase as the voices came closer. Nolan's shirt remained open. Another two or three floors and they'd be caught. What was wrong with him?

"I don't want to be anywhere near you."

He chuckled as he finger-combed his hair, which she'd mussed dragging her own fingers through the sleek sable strands. "Yeah, I could tell." He bent to retrieve her briefcase. "I'll see you tonight."

"I have plans," she said. Not a lie exactly, but she wasn't about to tell him her evening would been spent drinking bad coffee at an AA meeting in the Marina District's community center basement.

"I have a dinner meeting with clients," he said as if she'd never spoken, "but I'll stop by afterward. Around eleven?"

"Don't bother." She snatched her case from him, then glanced nervously upward as the voices became more distinct. "I'm going out of town," she said, deciding at that precise moment to take advantage of the trip she'd won at the fund-raiser.

She inched closer to the door. Another foot and a half and she'd be free, if her weak legs continued to hold. Her knees were trembling so hard, navigation in a pair of heels wasn't only a challenge but a hazard to her health. She reached the door and nearly sighed in relief.

"Mikki, wait," he said as she yanked open the heavy door. "You can't—"

"What I can or can't do is no longer your concern," she reminded him heatedly, then narrowly escaped discovery.

She glanced at her watch as she hurried toward the elevators. "Dammit," she muttered. She'd never make across town to the Sea Breeze on time now. "Thank you, Nolan."

She pressed the call button, then let out a sharp gasp when she caught sight of her reflection in the polished brass panel. Thank God the lobby was momentarily deserted. With her hair in wild disarray, lipstick smeared over swollen, just-kissed lips, clothes rumpled and her skirt twisted around so the back zipper was off center in the front, it wouldn't take a genius to guess what she'd been up to.

She told herself she didn't care. After all, she was well past the age of consent. Her only problem stemmed from the fact that for her, wisdom had little to do with age, not when sex entered the equation.

Or more appropriately, not when Nolan and sex entered the equation, she thought suddenly. Because no matter how often she tried to tell herself he was all wrong for her, she didn't doubt for a second he'd always be her greatest weakness.

"GOOD CALL. I owe you one," Nolan said to his assistant.

Ozzie Parish grinned, obviously pleased with himself. "Didn't I tell you Eckerd would deny the motion?"

Nolan dropped his briefcase on the floor by his desk. "Yeah, you did," he agreed, taking the handful of pink message slips Ozzie held out for him.

Ozzie clicked his tongue and crossed Nolan's corner office to pluck a few dry leaves from the potted plants on the brass plant stand near the bank of windows overlooking the city. "So," Ozzie prompted, "how did the missus take the court's decision?"

Nolan chuckled at the memory of Mikki's outrage. "Not well." A gross understatement. If she'd been within reach of a sharp instrument, she'd have sliced him up and gleefully fed him to the sea lions in the bay.

All that fiery passion aimed in his direction had been a huge turn-on, and although he probably hadn't helped his cause, Mikki remained a temptation he wasn't about to resist. Thankfully she was equally tempted, and he planned to exploit that fact as often as necessary until he convinced her she couldn't live without him.

"Schedule Connie Hillman for an appointment next week, would you, Oz?"

"Will do." Ozzie made a note on his steno pad, then gave Nolan a once-over. "No missing parts, I see. I'm impressed."

"Don't be," Nolan said. "I can handle my wife."

He circled the desk and sat in the buttery-soft leather chair. After flipping through the messages collected while he'd been in court all morning, he gave Ozzie a list of files he wanted pulled from central filing. Prior to the motion before Eckerd, he'd attended a brief hearing on a custody matter, plus another settlement conference in the Hillman divorce. The division of property still hadn't been resolved after three attempts, and today the judge had reached the limit of her patience. She'd ordered the parties to come to a mutually acceptable resolution within thirty days or she would hold them each in contempt and levy a hefty fine, a threat that his client's husband, the cheap Zachary Hillman, would hopefully take seriously.

Ozzie dropped into the chair across from Nolan's desk. "Then old man Turner should be a breeze," he said slyly.

Nolan looked at Ozzie. "What do you mean?"

"He's waiting to see you."

"He's here?" Robert Turner was *the* Turner of Turner, Crawford and Lowe. "Why didn't you say something sooner?"

Ozzie appeared mildly sheepish. "Sorry, boss man."

"Did he say what he wanted?"

Ozzie shook his head. "He flew in from L.A. this morning and just showed up, asking for you."

"A phone call wouldn't suffice?"

Ozzie shrugged his wiry shoulders. "Guess not."

"And he didn't say what he wanted?" Nolan confirmed again.

"Not a word."

Nolan let out a sigh and stood, dropping the remainder of unread messages on his desk. "Let him know I'm on my way," he told Ozzie, and promptly left his office.

Turner's sudden appearance couldn't be good news, Nolan thought. Something had to be up if the old man had flown to San Francisco just to speak with him personally. Maybe they were yanking the partnership away from him because of the unresolved issues with the divorce. Although he'd been acting in the capacity of managing partner, he hadn't yet signed the final partnership agreement. Perhaps they viewed his marital status as a liability. As partner, he held a certain fiduciary responsibility to the firm. California was a community property state, which entitled Mikki to half of his assets. Because he'd known it would infuriate his old man, he hadn't asked Mikki to sign a standard prenuptial agreement, either. They were still legally married, which entitled her to half of everything he owned, including his interest in the firm.

He took the elevator to the penthouse suite the firm maintained for the use of the three founding partners whenever they were in town. He didn't believe Mikki would ever to pull such a low-end stunt. Her fierce independent streak hadn't even allowed her to accept spousal support when they'd separated. He'd sent the checks anyway at first, and she'd ripped each of them to shreds and mailed back the remains.

The elevator door slid open and he walked into the foyer of the elegant penthouse suite with its lush taupe carpet and antique mahogany furnishings. Robert Turner sat in an emerald damask wing chair, a ridiculously delicate china cup and saucer perched on the round table beside him, a copy of *California Lawyer* open on his lap.

Nolan cleared his throat.

Turner glanced up from the magazine article he'd been reading and motioned for Nolan to take a seat. "Nolan," he said in greeting. "Good of you to come. Coffee?"

As if he'd had a choice in the matter, Nolan thought, crossing the room to the sofa. "No, thank you." He leaned back and tried to appear relaxed, as if being summoned to the penthouse was a common component of his day. "I'm fine."

Turner closed the magazine and set it on the coffee table in front of Nolan. "Settling in all right?"

"Yes," Nolan answered, glancing down at the magazine, his gaze zeroing in on an unlabeled manila folder. "Just fine. The staff has been more than accommodating."

"Good," Turner nodded. "No other problems? Concerns?"

"No," Nolan answered, wondering where the conversation was heading. "None whatsoever."

"Good. Good to hear." Turner smiled as if it were expected of him more than any genuine display of emotion or pleasure. "And how is the Delaney matter progressing?"

Nolan relaxed considerably. His client, Amelia Ferguson, Zoe Delaney's birth mother, was the wife of Bradley Ferguson, a prominent San Francisco entrepreneur and one of the firm's most valued clients.

"The court withheld ruling on our client's petition for custody until social services can complete a full investigation," he explained. "No less than I expected, but they did issue the injunction to stay the adoption. A Guardian ad Litem will be appointed, naturally, to represent the minor. I'm considering asking for supervised visitation for our client in the meantime."

Turner paused a moment to take a drink from that silly china cup. "We'd like to see this matter resolved quickly," he said meaningfully.

"I understand," Nolan told him. *Gotta keep the big-money client happy,* he thought sarcastically. "Maureen Baxter is the social worker involved, and an acquaintance. I'll see what I can do to help speed up the process." After the chunk of change he'd dropped into the building fund for Baxter House, he figured Maureen owed him at least one more favor.

Turner returned the cup to the saucer. "And how is that unfortunate business of your divorce from Ms. Correlli progressing?"

Nolan immediately stiffened. Turner might have posed the question in an offhand manner, but Nolan wasn't fooled by the old man's nonchalance. "As expected," he answered carefully. "Our motion to validate the proceeding was denied this morning."

Turner's slim silvery eyebrows angled downward in a frown. "Who was the judge?"

"Eckerd," Nolan told him, glancing again at the unmarked file. "Guess he's as by-the-book as they come." And the exact reason he'd taken Ozzie's advice and instructed his assistant to pull whatever strings necessary to get the hearing on Judge Eckerd's calendar.

"So I've heard." Turner looked at him with stone-cold hazel eyes. "This delay could present a problem, you know."

Oh, yeah, he knew all right, and it pissed him off. The Delaney custody matter had been a smoke screen for the real purpose of his summons to the penthouse. If the founding partners were prepared to pull the partnership out from under him and return the mid-six-figure check he'd written as down payment without breaking a sweat, then Robert Turner, Thomas Crawford and Wills Lowe could pound sand for all he cared. With the money the buy-in was costing him, he could just as well strike out on his own and hang his own shingle.

"We were hoping the issue with Ms. Correlli would be resolved by now," Turner said, his voice laden with disapproval.

"I don't anticipate any problems," Nolan told him,

careful to keep his irritation hemmed. "Michaela is anxious to have the matter concluded." A fact she'd made patently clear on several occasions.

"This does cause us concern," Turner continued. "Considering Ms. Correlli's history, I'm sure you can understand why we would prefer to proceed with an abundance of caution before finalizing the partnership agreement."

Nolan frowned. Sanctimonious bastard, he thought. "No, I don't understand," he said. What the hell difference did it make if Mikki came from modest means? Her parents had died when she was little more than a toddler, and she didn't even remember them. With no other living relatives to assume her care, she'd become a ward of the state. He knew she'd spent some time in juvenile facilities and a series of foster homes until she'd been placed with Emma when she was twelve, but since when did being born poor or orphaned raise concern?

Turner indicated the unlabeled folder on the coffee table. "Our investigation revealed certain facts that lead us to believe Ms. Correlli could cause difficulties for you, and quite possibly the firm. Financially speaking."

"Even if Mikki did exercise her legal right to half of my assets, which I have no reason to believe she ever would, I can afford it," he said, his voice hard. He glanced pointedly at the folder on the table. "What I want to know is why you had my wife investigated without telling me about it?"

One of Turner's silvery eyebrows rose a fraction, but Nolan didn't give a damn if he'd offended him. If the founding partners didn't trust him enough to tell him they'd planned to poke around in Mikki's background, then they could kiss him, and his money, goodbye.

"Standard procedure," Turner explained, dismissing Nolan's concern. "However, under the circumstances, I'm sure you'll understand if we choose to wait until the matter has been sufficiently resolved before finalizing your status as a full partner. In the interim, you'll maintain your position as head of the family law division here in San Francisco, of course."

Anger vibrated through him. "Of course," Nolan said, his voice dripping with sarcasm.

"Our discussion here today will remain private," Turner continued as if Nolan hadn't spoken. "This is not a reflection of your abilities or our desire to have you as a partner in the firm, Nolan. Please don't misunderstand our intent. We feel it is a necessary precaution under the circumstances, and we must protect the firm first."

"Under *what* circumstances?" Nolan demanded angrily. "Mikki might have grown up poor, but she's not what you're thinking. She's too independent to ask for a dime of my money." He shot Turner a heated look. "Or the firm's."

Turner sighed heavily. "You misunderstand," he said. "Ms. Correlli's childhood isn't at issue, or her circumstances. Our concern is the alcoholism and the liability issues involved."

Alcoholism? What the hell...

He shook his head. "No," he said vehemently. "Not Mikki. It's not possible." So she sometimes drank to excess, so did he, but who didn't on occasion? No, not a chance. Mikki was too much of a control freak to succumb to any addiction. It simply wasn't possible.

Or was it?

He recalled the time they'd gone to a party at Tucker's brother's place and she'd started pounding shots with him and Tuck. She'd matched them shot for shot until the three of them were all faded, but he couldn't remember her touching another drop for weeks.

Until the next time when she'd gotten drunk fairly quickly, but she'd told him she'd skipped lunch and the alcohol had gone straight to her head. She hadn't always drank when they'd been out with friends, so he'd believed her. Hell, he'd even teased her about being a lightweight. He couldn't remember her ever drinking anything stronger than coffee or soda at home, so he'd never once considered that she might have a problem with booze. Had there ever been an occasion when Mikki hadn't ended up wasted whenever they'd been out drinking?

"No," he said again, but with much less conviction. "There's been a mistake."

Robert Turner's expression softened. "I'm sorry, Nolan. There's been no mistake. Ms. Correlli was ordered to spend twenty-eight days in a rehabilitation facility. It's all there," he said, once again indicating the unmarked file. "I do understand she's been successful in maintaining her sobriety for the past four years, which is commendable. But, if she should have a setback…"

Four years? Right around the time he went to Mexico to file for—

…*divorcing you nearly killed me.*

Nolan's heart plummeted. Finally he understood why she kept insisting she wanted nothing to do with him. God, if he'd known he would've…what? Come running back to her? The man he was today wouldn't hesitate. The selfish prick he'd been five years ago, the one more interested in salvaging his pride than his marriage, wasn't anywhere near as confident he'd have made the right decision.

"You're sure about this?" he asked, praying Turner was mistaken, but knowing in his gut the old man spoke the truth.

Turner's nod was solemn. "I do apologize, Nolan," the older man said in an uncharacteristic display of genuine sympathy. "I didn't realize you were unaware your wife is a recovering alcoholic."

8

"NOLAN IS THE *WHAT*?"

"Counsel for the petitioner," Maureen Baxter repeated. "Oh, come on, Mikki. Something like this was bound to happen now that he's back in town."

Of course, but a girl could hope otherwise, couldn't she? Fat lot of good it'd done her, though.

The double-caramel-swirl cheesecake she'd ordered suddenly tasted like cardboard. She'd needed something to soothe her after her encounter with Nolan in the stairwell, and had opted for the relative safety of a sugar high. She set her fork on the plate and spread her napkin over the half-eaten dessert as if she were covering a dead body at a crime scene.

She glanced at Maureen, the epitome of cool elegance, wondering if beneath that sleek, polished exterior lurked a fellow conspirator in the plot to turn her life completely upside and keep it there. "Okay, so tell me, whose ass do I have to kiss to have the case reassigned to the next advocate on the rotation? I'm not taking this one. I can't."

I can't be around Nolan and not have sex with him.

"Zoe Delaney needs the best, and you and I both know that's you. *I* need you on this one. More importantly, Zoe needs you," Maureen said.

Tension knotted Mikki's neck. Fingers of pain crawled up the back of her skull followed immediately by a dull, rhythmic throb. "I truly despise you right now," she told her colleague and friend, but Maureen just smiled smugly.

Mikki dug through her purse for aspirin to ease the pain.

"Stop sulking," Maureen chided with a gentle laugh, signaling the waitress for more iced tea. "I know you'll get over it eventually."

Mikki looked up from the useless search of her purse. "I'll consider it an act of good faith toward the major sucking up this is going to cost you if you'll hook me up with some aspirin."

"You're in luck." Maureen quickly produced a small bottle of aspirin.

Mikki washed a couple down with her refilled glass of iced tea, then pulled a fresh yellow legal pad from her briefcase and set it on the table in front of her. "Damned pathetic when a couple of painkillers are the best thing that's happened to a girl in a week." Well, other than a pretty incredible orgasm and an almost orgasm. If only they hadn't been interrupted...

"That bad?"

"Yes, actually," Mikki said, taking advantage of the sympathetic look in Maureen's eyes. "It sucks to be me right now."

Maureen handed her a thick file. "Don't be such a drama queen," her friend teased.

"Ha! You want drama? Where should I start? How about with finding out my ex-husband *isn't*. That's drama."

Maureen had the courtesy to wince. "So I've heard," she said. "Tucker Schulz mentioned something about it when I met with him at Baxter House earlier this week. Oh, did I tell you he's donating the electrical work?"

"Congratulations," Mikki said, not feeling particularly charitable at the moment. "Did I tell you Judge Eckerd refused to validate the divorce, which means I have the joy of facing the humiliation of a failed marriage a second time. And as a bonus, one of my closest friends—" she shot Maureen an accusing look "—stoops to emotional blackmail so I'll represent the minor in a custody matter with my *not* ex-husband as counsel for the petitioner. Still think I'm being overly dramatic?"

Maureen slid a lock of silky, mink-colored, shoulder-length hair behind her ear. "Just a little. But the role of victim still doesn't suit you."

"Tell me about it," Mikki said, and frowned. She didn't know why she expected understanding from Maureen when her own sisters hadn't been sympathetic when she'd had lunch with them yesterday. All she'd told them was maybe she should just drag Nolan to bed and get it over with, and they'd started in on her with that fate crap again. Even her mom hadn't offered her the usual shoulder to whine on when she'd called her last night. If one more person suggested she and Nolan were meant to be together, she'd scream.

Maureen tilted her head slightly to the side as she regarded Mikki thoughtfully for a moment. "But that isn't what's really got your thong in a twist over Nolan, is it?"

Nolan had had her thong twisted rather nicely earlier. And that, Mikki readily concluded, was her problem. They might not be destined to ride off into the sunset together, but they were definitely headed toward something…like the nearest bed. Or stairwell, she thought, feeling a rush of heat creep into her cheeks.

"Save the counseling session for someone more in need," she told Maureen. "Or who gives a damn."

"Know what I think?"

Mikki let out a long-suffering sigh. "No," she said, "and I don't want to hear it. I've gotten enough opinions on my marital status from Emma, Rory and Lauren to last me the rest of the decade."

"Tough." Maureen grinned in that calculating way she had. "You're going to hear it anyway because I care about you. You're not in a pissy mood because of what's going on with Nolan, but because you blew over four years of sobriety Friday night. I dare you to tell me I'm wrong."

Mikki looked away and considered leaving. She almost regretted never telling Maureen about her alcoholism. But when Maureen had confided in her a couple of years ago about the problems in her own marriage because of her then-husband's drinking problem, Mikki had urged her long-time friend to attend Al-Anon meetings, a support group for family members of alcoholics. Because of her own father's alcoholism, Mikki knew the effects it could have on a person's life. Just gather her things and walk out of the Sea Breeze Café as fast as humanly possible. She could review the Delaney file on her own. Maureen's summaries were always meticulously detailed anyway. Over lunch they'd brought each other up to speed on the cases scheduled for hearings next week and had even discussed the progress on Baxter House. She did not need anyone to remind her of how stupidly she'd behaved Friday night at the fund-raiser. She'd been doing enough of that herself. Dwelling on her mistake wasn't as conducive to her sobriety as focusing on the strength that had kept her sober for four years, but it sure made it easier to throw a pity party.

Maureen reached over and rested her hand on Mikki's in a gesture of comfort. "Stop blaming him, Mikki. He didn't pour that booze down your throat. You managed that all on your own."

Mikki tugged her hand away, feeling cornered. She wanted to run, but her inability to face the truth until it was too late always seemed to be what landed her in the most trouble. "Butt out, Baxter," she warned.

Maureen straightened. Her lips pulling into a thin line and a hard-as-steel glint entering her eyes. "Are you at least attending AA meetings again?"

"What to do you think?" Mikki fired back defensively.

"Good. Then accept responsibility for your actions and move forward. One day at a time."

If Maureen recited the Serenity Prayer next, Mikki swore she'd hurl. She crossed her arms and glared at her friend. "Gee, thank you, Dr. Phil. I didn't know that."

"Oh, stuff the tough routine, Mikki. I know what you're going through, remember." Despite the hardness of her tone, Maureen's gaze softened with the compassion of someone who'd walked a similar path, only not as an addict but as the former spouse of one. "You're not alone."

Mikki exhaled a lengthy sigh and managed a tentative smile. "I know, and I'm sorry. But if this is your idea of sucking up—" she forced her grin to widen a fraction "—your technique bites."

"So I'll work on it." Maureen returned her smile. "Now, do you want to talk about your new client?"

Relieved to be discussing a subject other than her own failings, Mikki nodded and poised her pen over the legal pad. "Shoot."

"Everything you need is in there." Maureen indicated the file she'd handed Mikki earlier. "We have custody at issue in a stayed adoption proceeding. The medical records are extensive, but they've been summarized in detail for you. I'll have the actual records sent to your office by next Tuesday."

Mikki nodded. "Tell me about Zoe."

"She's a sweet girl. For a nine-year-old she has a pretty good head on her shoulders. Considering everything this poor kid has been subjected to," Maureen added with a regretful shake of her head. "Well, her progress is amazing. She'll be in counseling for a number of years yet, but you'll see what I mean when you meet with her and the Michaelsons. I've set up a tentative meeting for Wednesday afternoon. Check your calendar and let me know if that works for you."

Mikki made a note of the meeting time, then set her pen on the legal pad. Reaching for her glass of tea, she asked, "The Michaelsons?"

"Zoe's foster parents," Maureen explained. "They've had the girl in therapy since we placed her with them two years ago. Those twice weekly sessions, combined with John and Bobbie's patience, have been key to Zoe's progress."

Just as Emma had been key to hers, Mikki thought suddenly. And Lauren's, Maureen's and a number of other foster kids over the years.

"Zoe could be a success story, if we can keep her with the Michaelsons. She's one tough little survivor."

Maureen's word choice had Mikki tensing all over again. *Survivor.* She'd used the description countless times to label the victims of abuse she represented, but it never lost its impact. Opposing counsel accused her of spouting the term to garner the court's sympathy, but she knew differently. Kids like Zoe *were* survivors, and she had zero patience for anyone who dismissed her young clients, or what they'd suffered, so callously. Hell would be a more apt description of what some of those kids faced.

Mikki picked up her pen again. "Which parent has filed the petition for custody?"

"The mother. Father's deceased." Maureen's expression turned grim. "Jailhouse justice."

"So the father was convicted on charges of child abuse?" Even murderers, drug dealers and thugs couldn't stomach someone hurting little kids, often handing out their own form of punishment. Depending on the severity of the crime, sometimes under the watchful eye of a prison guard.

Maureen nodded. "Delaney was convicted on numerous counts of sexual assault on a minor, battery, neglect, prostituting a minor, just to name a few. It's all in the file."

"Son of a bitch," Mikki muttered under her breath. Fierce outrage slammed into her so hard, her hands went clammy. The pen slipped from her fingers and clattered to the table.

Maureen caught the pen before it rolled off the edge. "A real deviate," she said, her tone vehement.

"That's not the term I'd use," Mikki said, willing her hands to stop trembling. Too many in her line of work had hardened themselves to the ugliness of their job, but not her. Anger. Frustration. Her emotions ran the gamut over every damaged child she represented, but nothing rocked her harder than cases like Zoe Delaney's. They were always the toughest for her and never failed to drain her. As difficult as her job could be, she figured these kids needed someone on their side, so it might as well be someone like her who had too real an understanding of what they were going through.

"It's not the term anyone involved in this case has used, either," Maureen said dryly.

"Where was the mother when he was…" Her emotions were such a tangle, she couldn't bring herself to vocalize what the bastard had done to his own daughter. "Where was the mother?"

"Gone," Maureen said. "Zoe was only two years old when her birth mother, Amelia, abandoned her. There was a long history of spousal abuse, but the last time Delaney beat her so badly, she'd spent months in traction, her jaw surgically reconstructed. She claims she was afraid of what he'd do to her if she pressed charges, and there is evidence she did attempt to press charges on two prior occasions, which were dropped, of course."

"Of course," Mikki mumbled.

"When she was released from the hospital, she ran and didn't stop until she hit the Florida Keys," Maureen said. "Delaney had already threatened her family, her friends, and told them if she tried to see Zoe, he'd make sure the girl disappeared for good. Amelia alleges she took this to mean he'd kill Zoe, so she never tried to gain custody."

Mikki leaned forward and gave her friend a hard stare. "I know and understand the issues involved with battered wife syndrome, but I have no sympathy for a woman who leaves her kid with a goddamned monster. You know I'll nail this woman hard. That's why you wanted me on this case, isn't it?"

Maureen had the decency to appear somewhat guilty. "Yes," she admitted. "I know it was low, but, Mikki, this woman can't be awarded custody. She hasn't seen Zoe in over seven years."

Mikki wasn't thrilled with Maureen's tactics and resented her taking advantage of their close friendship, but she wouldn't allow it to prevent her from doing the best job she knew how to protect Zoe.

Mikki straightened. "I'm assuming Zoe doesn't remember her mother."

"That's part of the problem," Maureen agreed. "Zoe's come so far in such a short time, my concern is what kind of setback she could endure if she's removed from the first real home where she's ever felt safe."

"I'll be damned if that's going to happen," Mikki said. "And Nolan is actually representing this woman? Why? Any custody issues I've ever known him to take on were all directly related to divorce proceedings. This isn't the type of case he usually handles."

"I don't know that he has a choice," Maureen said. "The mother is now Bradley Ferguson's wife. They met about four years ago when he was vacationing in the Keys. They married a few months later and he brought her back to San Francisco to live. She alleges she did attempt to contact her ex-husband for visitation after returning to the Bay area."

"I doubt it," Mikki scoffed. "First off, is there a petition to modify visitation or custody on file with the family court?"

"No," Maureen said. "And it doesn't make sense to

me, either, especially if she was as terrified of Delaney as she claims."

"Then why come back to San Francisco at all?"

"She's a Ferguson now," Maureen said. "Delaney didn't exactly move in the same circle she married into, so the chances of running into him on Russian Hill were slim. Plus, by the time she says she tried to contact Delaney, he'd already been in custody awaiting trial, and Zoe had been in our system for a couple of years already. It doesn't add up."

"Sounds like a cock-and-bull story she made up to cover her sorry butt with Ferguson," Mikki said, signaling the waitress for the check. "I'm sure her new sugar daddy wouldn't think too highly of someone who never planned to rescue her own kid from a piece of scum like Delaney. The fact that she didn't come forward until after the notices were published would support that argument."

"Possibly," Maureen agreed, and began to gather her things. "We have no record of contact by the mother with our office until after the public notices were published by the Michaelsons' attorney once they initiated the adoption proceedings. Nolan's office has filed an injunction, so the adoption has already been stayed until the issue of custody is resolved."

"Won't happen," Mikki said as she slid from the booth. "I won't let it." She looked at Maureen and shook her head. "I still can't believe Nolan actually took this case."

Maureen laughed as she stood, but the sound held

more bitterness than humor. "Oh, I can," she said. "Ferguson is one of Turner, Crawford and Lowe's biggest clients. They represent most, if not all, of his interests. Don't be surprised if Nolan is under pressure to play hardball on this one."

Mikki let out a huff of breath. "He hasn't seen hardball," she scoffed, wondering what it would be like to go up against Nolan in court. She supposed she should be a tiny bit concerned. He was a damned good lawyer, but then, so was she.

Mikki took care of the bill and left the restaurant with Maureen. "Don't worry," she said once they were outside, hoping she wasn't projecting an overconfidence that would come back to bite her later. "When I get through with his client, not even Judge Eckerd will grant this woman custody. That's a promise."

"I hope you're right," Maureen said meaningfully. She smoothed her hair from her face and held it in place. "The Fergusons might be worth millions and can afford advantages the Michaelsons can't, but the Ferguson money can't give Zoe what John and Bobbie have."

"Which is?"

"Hope."

THE DRIVE OUT OF the city took Nolan longer than he'd anticipated. Even though he'd left San Francisco well after rush hour, crossing the bridge alone had cost him an hour. The dinner meeting with clients had concluded earlier than expected—in part, he suspected, because he was so distracted. Since Turner's blindsiding him with the disturbing news about Mikki, he'd thought of little else, and it showed.

Following his meeting, he'd driven straight to Mikki's, but the apartment had been deserted. Unable to get in touch with Rory, either at home or at any of the Lavender Field locations, he'd tried calling Lauren next. Appealing to Mikki's younger sister's romantic nature had been an underhanded ploy, but Lauren had ratted out Mikki's whereabouts easily enough that he didn't feel too guilty.

He'd packed a weekender bag and was halfway to Napa before he questioned his motives. Just what the hell did he think he was doing, anyway?

As he continued along the interstate to Napa Valley, he realized his mistake had been focusing solely on convincing Mikki she still wanted him rather than stopping long enough to really listen to what she'd been trying to tell him all along. He'd heard the words... They were no good for each other... It would never last... Get out of her life and stay out. He just hadn't *listened*.

Finally he understood. He didn't like it, but he got it. He wasn't proud of the fact it had taken a truckload of reality to run him down, either. If he'd been paying close enough to attention, he would've realized sooner Mikki's objections weren't a matter of her *not* loving him, but rather of her *fearing* her love for him.

Unfortunately fear wasn't something he could physically put his hands on to obliterate. When he'd been little, he'd been afraid of the dark, more so during his mother's periods of hospitalization. As an adult, he understood the dark hadn't been his problem, but insecurity caused by his mother's and father's long absences. Regardless of how often the closet door had been opened to prove there were no monsters hidden inside, he wouldn't go to sleep unless someone stayed with him.

He flipped on his blinker and changed lanes to pass an eighteen-wheeler. So, he thought, for him to conquer Mikki's fear, he'd have to understand the cause to know what made her feel safe. Problem solved.

Yeah, right. Considering how well you two communicate, that ought to be a piece of cake.

He blew out a stream of breath. His conscience had a point. And what about her alcoholism? Was that somehow rooted in fear, as well?

According to the information Turner's investigator had unearthed, Mikki had been sober since rehab. He didn't consider it a coincidence that the night he'd told her they were still married was the night she'd chucked four years of sobriety out the window.

The reason she hadn't gone to Mexico herself and had hired the first shyster she'd found in the phone book finally made sense to him. What he couldn't understand, though, was if she was really so anxious to be rid of him why she hadn't spoken up in court this morning. She could've requested a side bar to avoid the shame and embarrassment of having to explain herself in open court. Eckerd might be a stickler for rules, but he wasn't insensitive. If Mikki had explained why she'd been unable to travel to Mexico, how she'd been unable to hire competent counsel to represent her, Judge Eckerd might have granted the motion. Regardless of the circumstances, she'd had an acceptable, legitimate excuse.

Which, Nolan thought, meant she never had any intention of telling him she was an alcoholic. Shame? Perhaps, he thought, but he couldn't help wondering what else his wife had been keeping from him.

When had her problem with drinking started? When had it become uncontrollable? And why, for that matter? Now that he knew what to look for, he did realize she had exhibited classic symptoms of the disease during their marriage, but he hadn't seen it then. Or maybe he hadn't wanted to see it.

He hated himself for not noticing the signs sooner, hated that he'd left her alone to battle the disease. He couldn't say her problem didn't matter to him, because it did. Not in that it lessened his feelings for her, but because he loved her. He'd never stopped, and he had a feeling the only reason she'd even said she hadn't loved him in the first place was to hide the truth from him. But *why* was what he wanted to know. Was it just the alcoholism she was hiding or was there something more that he hadn't figured out? What wasn't he seeing?

He took the Napa exit and headed west to Highway 29. No matter how much Mikki might argue they stood no chance of a reconciliation, she was dead wrong. Sure, they had hurdles to navigate, the most treacherous being whatever the hell she was so damned afraid of that kept her pushing him away.

A smile kicked up the corners of his mouth. Loving Mikki wasn't always easy, but when two people were as combustible as they were, there were bound to be a few fireworks now and then.

That thought had him ignoring the posted speed limit and pressing his foot down on the accelerator. Within minutes he had his BMW tucked away in the guest parking lot of the Valley Inn Bed and Breakfast and a key card to the Champagne Suite in his hand, courtesy of an accommodating desk clerk, once he provided her with proof of his share of the prize he and Mikki had won at the key party.

With only an ounce or two of apprehension, he took the elegant staircase to the second level. He expected a full out battle when he told her he had no intention of leaving until they reached a resolution—preferably one that had her moving into the house on Telegraph Hill. The sooner, the better.

He found the door to her suite and slid the card into the lock. The green light flashed and he smiled. Mikki would definitely declare war, but then, he'd always admired her passion. Tonight, he thought as he entered the room, he wasn't above using it against her to get what he wanted from her—and nothing short of forever would suffice.

9

MIKKI RESTED HER HEAD against the bath pillow and closed her eyes, concentrating on the steaming jets of water pulsating against her skin. Eventually she started to relax and the anxiety slowly eased from her body. Without a doubt, today had been one of the top five worst on record. She should've been forewarned when the heel of her favorite pair of red pumps snapped off before she'd even made it out of her apartment this morning that she was destined for disaster.

Adding insult to injury, while enduring three hours of horrendous traffic to escape the city, an SUV had cut her off and she spilled her caramel latte all over the passenger seat of her car, staining the seat and her new canvas overnight bag.

She emitted a soft moan of exhausted pleasure as the whirlpool worked its magic on the taut muscles in her neck, back and shoulders. She wiggled her toes beneath the water and sighed. Oh, yes, this was exactly what she needed.

Well, almost, she amended. No matter how bad for her in the long run, she would've preferred a much more physically gratifying method of ridding her body of tension, but since she hadn't invited Nolan to join her, that wasn't about to happen.

She opened her eyes, certain she'd heard a noise. The click of a door in the distance, perhaps? She strained to hear more. The only sound she registered was the constant humming whir of the whirlpool tub's motor.

Aromatic steam from the melon-scented bath oil she'd added to the water rose around her. She pushed away a few damp tendrils of hair clinging to her face, then reached for the glass she'd set on the ceramic tile ledge surrounding the tub. The Valley Inn Bed and Breakfast boasted one of the most premiere wine cellars in Napa, and rather than sampling the award-winning wines, she'd been content to quench her thirst with a diet soda.

She set her glass on the ledge, settled back into the tub and closed her eyes. Coming to Napa had been the best thing she could've done for herself. She'd felt a desperate need to get away from the city, from the memories and from Nolan. Peace and quiet. Clear her head. Think about what to do next. Develop a solid game plan. She needed all that, plus a damned strong offense—fast—if she hoped to successfully survive the next few months until her divorce was finalized.

The new case Maureen had brought her today had definitely upset her, but she knew that not all of her anxiety was tangled up in the memories Zoe Delaney's story had raised in Mikki. It was the realization she'd be forced to spend time with Nolan when she needed to keep her contact with him to an absolute minimum. In the week since he'd reappeared in her life, they'd been together exactly four times. During each of those encounters, neither one of them could keep their hands to themselves. How was a girl supposed to maintain her sanity and that all-important emotional distance when she couldn't be within ten feet of the man without rubbing up against him and purring like an damned alley cat in heat?

For pity's sake, she thought, it wasn't as if she'd deprived herself sexually since their separation, yet she wouldn't know it by the way she behaved around Nolan. She'd taken more than a handful of lovers since the separation, but always on her terms. Those liaisons rarely lasted long and for her were nothing more than a means to a sexually gratifying end. She was no stranger to the occasional one night stand, but the truth was, the men she slept with usually bored her silly.

She didn't necessarily jump into the sack with just anyone that came along. She did have her standards. But there was no arguing the fact that once a man served his usefulness, she never looked back.

She knew the problem was that she hadn't found a man who could really hold her interest the way Nolan always had. She honestly doubted such a man even existed. Oh, she'd had some laughs with a few, but in general, longevity simply wasn't her style. Three months marked the longest relationship she'd had with any man since her so-called divorce.

Nolan had never bored her. He'd infuriated her

plenty, just as she'd ticked him off on numerous occasions. She'd been livid the time he'd taken off with Tuck and one of his brothers to Lake Tahoe for a guys-only weekend and hadn't bothered to call to let her know they'd been delayed because the transmission had gone on Tuck's pickup. They were supposed to be home Sunday evening, but by Monday night no one had heard a word from the guys. When Nolan finally walked through the door after midnight, he'd been greeted by a few choice words from his wife. He had remembered to call home in the future, though.

She smoothed her hair away from her face and frowned. They hadn't always argued, and the memories of happier times during their marriage were priceless to her. He'd brought her canned chicken soup, juice, lilacs and the latest issue of *Cosmo* when she was sick with a cold, and chocolate when she'd had a rough day.

She used to pick out his ties because he never could remember what suits he had in the closet. He would sometimes buy her skimpy panties because he said it made him hot thinking about her wearing them.

She'd surprise him with bags of licorice-flavored jelly beans, and if he wasn't working late checking points and authorities of appellate briefs or researching specific points of law, he would bring her something from Felucca's Deli whenever she'd been stuck at work. A few times they'd been alone and made love right in her office.

A smile tilted her lips as she remembered the time he'd papered the entire bottom of her briefcase with yellow sticky notes complete with written graphic detail of various sexual positions. She'd been in court when she'd discovered the notes, and had nearly died of embarrassment when one had somehow become stuck between the pages of a motion she'd filed with the clerk.

Oh yes, she thought. Nolan definitely stimulated her. Mind, body and spirit—especially body, she thought with a silly little sigh of remembered pleasure.

They'd been awaiting bar results and weren't making much money, so dinner at a fancy restaurant to celebrate their first wedding anniversary had been out of the question. While she'd been at work, Nolan had improvised and raided her mom's place for the supplies he'd needed to transform their cramped living room into a makeshift supper club using a card table and borrowed china.

Rose petals from her mom's garden and a few homemade scented candles had perfumed the air while they'd dined on grilled burgers and cheap wine. Afterward they'd danced to love songs on the radio and made love until dawn. One of the few times, she thought, that she hadn't drank to excess.

If it weren't for that damned insane need of his to procreate, they might never have separated, despite his taking the job in L.A. without consulting her first. She hadn't been too thrilled when she'd learned the job required a relocation six hundred miles away from the only real family she'd ever known, but she'd loved him and would have coped with long-distance bills, e-mail and supersaver fares. But when he'd laid that whole stay-home-and-make-babies crap on her, she'd panicked.

She couldn't have children. Period. Not only was her drinking problem becoming harder to control, but she was a Correlli, and she wasn't willing to risk bringing a child into the world if even the slimmest possibility existed that she would cause a child irreparable harm. While she understood on a conscious level that, despite the odds, not all victims of abuse abused, that possibility still didn't alleviate her fears. Maybe she wouldn't physically hurt a child the way she'd been hurt, but what if she, like her mother, suddenly didn't want to be a parent? Or what if she finally lost her battle with booze, the way she had done anyway? Mikki knew how it felt to be abandoned, how if felt to be hurt by the person who was supposed to protect you from harm. She didn't want a child to be subjected to a single ounce of the horrors she'd suffered.

If she'd been brave enough to tell Nolan the truth at the start of their relationship, that she'd lied to him about her parents being dead so he wouldn't learn what had happened to her, maybe, just maybe, they could've stayed together. But she'd panicked, she'd pushed him away because in her mind, he'd deserved so much more than she was capable of giving. Regardless of how much she'd loved him, she'd always be a woman with a trainload of baggage that made it impossible for her to give him what he always wanted—a family.

She sat up suddenly. There it was again, a soft thud

this time. She tried to peer around the bathroom door she'd left ajar, but from what little view she had of the luxurious suite, she saw no cause for alarm. Still, she had the distinct impression she was no longer alone.

"Get over yourself," she muttered, and made a sound of disgust as she settled back into the relaxing warmth of the whirlpool. She was edgy, was all. And being ridiculous, she chastised herself. Other than her family, no one knew she'd taken off for Napa.

"So," she whispered. "What do we do now?"

Nolan was back in town for good, so unless she planned to follow through on her threat to relocate to Siberia, there was no easy solution. Although she'd eliminate the marriage nuisance when she filed for divorce, her brilliant, albeit brief, plan to limit contact hadn't lasted as long as the Super Bowl half-time show now that she'd been appointed Guardian ad Litem for Zoe Delaney. With Nolan representing her client's birth mother, they'd be crossing paths, and swords, often.

In some ways she felt as if she were starting over again. Each time she saw him, it became more and more difficult for her to summon the emotional distance required to survive the aftermath of him. And she knew from experience, Nolan Baylor was one tough habit to kick. Even now her skin grew tight just thinking about him.

Disgusted by her weakness for him, she stood and pushed the lever to drain the tub, then turned on the shower and washed her hair. By the time she emerged, the restlessness had increased, her body all achy and needy for his touch.

"Damn him," she muttered to her reflection as she combed the tangles from her hair. She blew most of it dry, then tamed the curls with gel before rubbing melon-scented lotion into her skin. From her latte-stained over-night bag, she pulled out a deep wine-colored chemise and slipped it over her head. The whisper-thin silk drifted over her curves, lightly caressing her skin, amplifying that tight, achy feeling she feared would plague her all night.

She knew she should've packed her vibrator.

Two steps into the bedroom suite and she came up short, staring in stunned disbelief. She blinked, but the image remained. Was the gorgeous male sitting on the edge of the frilly Victorian four-poster canopied bed with his arms propped on his knees a wishful figment of her overactive imagination or a heaven-sent, flesh-and-blood reality?

She prayed for reality.

Nolan wore the same gray Armani trousers from that morning, his crisp white dress shirt was rumpled and his tie was loose and hung haphazardly at a slight angle around his neck. Lines fanned from his eyes, the dark brown orbs underscored with fatigue. Even though he looked more than a little rough around the edges, her pulse still took off like a runner in the one hundred meter. Her nipples puckered and rasped against her silk chemise.

She swore, the single syllable sharp and distinct. She didn't ask him what he was doing in her suite, how he'd found her or even why he'd shown up, because she instinctively knew his coming here had been inevitable.

They were inevitable.

He looked up at her with that sexy, half smile she'd always loved turning up the corner of his mouth. "Hi, honey," he said lamely. "I'm home."

She should throw him out and save herself further heartache while she still had the chance. But why? Not only had her ability to resist him all but evaporated, she had wanting this since that night at Clementine's. What good was constant deprivation, anyway, when all it did was magnify her weakness for him? Did she really have anything to gain by denying the needs of her body, other than more restless, sleepless nights?

She folded her arms and hiked up one eyebrow. "You're late," she told him.

To anyone who didn't know him as well as she did, the slight change in his body language would've gone unnoticed. But she was so in tune to him, she didn't miss the way his shoulders relaxed or how his eyes softened.

He straightened and held his hand out to her. "Traffic was terrible. Forgive me?"

Slowly she approached him, thinking he'd never looked more handsome or more dangerous to her heart. Maybe some truth existed in that whole-universe-getting-it-right thing. She didn't pretend to have all the answers, or even a few of them, but for now, the concerns of the universe were out of her radar range. All she wanted was for Nolan to make her forget everything wrong about them and to take them both to that place where they'd always gotten it right.

She let out a sigh and looped her arms around his neck. "I might."

He pulled her close, his hands dipping beneath the hem of her chemise to cup her backside. His smile turned wicked as soon as he realized she wasn't wearing panties. "Guess I'll have to make it up to you then, won't I?"

His fingers massaged her bottom, sending tingles chasing over her skin. She trembled and his eyes darkened with desire. Setting her knee onto the edge of the bed, she rubbed against the thick length of his erect penis. "I'm not in a very forgiving mood," she purred. "This could take some time, but—" she slid her knee along the length of him "—you do seem up to the challenge."

He pulled back to look at her. The tenderness in his eyes had her breath catching in her throat and started her heart pounding in a heavy rhythm.

"Are you sure?"

His question held far more significance than she was prepared to examine too closely, so she opted for a face-value translation. *"This,"* she said, hoping he caught her meaning, "is all I've ever been sure about."

Keeping her gaze locked with his, she parted her legs, then took hold of one of his hands still cupping her bottom and placed it between her legs. Her back arched from the lightening-quick flash of pleasure that jolted through her the instant his fingers separated her already slick folds to tease her swollen, throbbing bud.

"Is the evidence sufficient, counselor?" she asked, her voice heavy with need.

He responded with a low, throaty growl of approval, then pushed his fingers inside her moist heat and slowly pumped with long, deep thrusts. Through the thin fabric of her chemise, his hot, wet mouth covered her nipple and he suckled her hard. Vivid sensation exploded inside her. The silk rasped her tender nipples in turn as he stroked and laved each of her breasts. With one hand he continued to stroke her from behind while he pushed into her with the other, keeping up the thrusts, each one easing deeper then withdrawing to spread the thick dew of her arousal over her folds. He filled her again, over and over, until her body pulled so tight with tension, she knew she couldn't withstand the exquisite torture much longer.

Her legs trembled. The climax he drove her to drew closer, closer...

He started to withdraw, but she grabbed his hand and held him to her, rocking her hips to heighten the pressure against her swollen clit. The fingers of his free hand entered her from behind and she came in a rush, the force of her orgasm wildly intense. She cried out, unintelligible sounds of pleasure intermingled with his name.

Heat raced through her veins, and it wasn't enough. She wanted more...always more.

"Don't stop," she rasped, her voice hoarse. "Make me hotter, Nolan. Make me come again so this feeling never ends."

He looked at her, his eyes blazing with hunger. "Tell me what you want."

"You know, dammit." She fisted her hand in his hair. "You're the only one who's ever known what I want."

He smiled lazily, then gently shifted her away and stood. With one tug, he had her chemise over her head and tossed aside. Grabbing hold of her hips, he turned her toward the bed, then bent her over until her hands gripped the edge of the mattress.

"Open for me." His voice was a rough, whispered demand that sent her senses spinning.

He didn't touch her, but she heard the rustle of fabric as he quickly undressed. "Spread your legs," he ordered. "Show me how wet you are for me, Mikki."

She did as he asked, parting her legs and lifting her bottom higher, opening herself to him. "I want you. I want you inside me. Now."

"Uh-uh," he said. "You wanted hotter, remember?"

She trembled from the anticipation humming along her nerve endings. Behind her, he traced his hand slowly down her spine. "First I'll make you so wet and hot, you can't stand it."

The sound of his voice had seriously cranked up her arousal gauge. The touch of his hands as he slid his fingertips along the seam of her bottom had her body temperature soaring.

"Only then will I give you want you want." His voice sounded strained, tight. "That's when I'll put my cock inside you and stroke you, just the way you've always liked it."

"Yes," she whispered when he pressed open her folds and pushed his fingers inside her still-sensitive flesh.

A low throaty growl rent the air and she had no idea which of them had made the sound. Already her senses were swimming amid a sea of sensual confusion from the highly charged state of arousal consuming her.

"You like it slow, don't you, Mikki? Long, slow and hard." His fingers illustrated the erotic picture her mind painted from his deep, sexy voice.

"Yes," she whispered. "I want you buried inside me, thick, hard and…" She let go of a deep moan of pleasure as renewed need rippled through her.

"And fast." He increased the tempo of his stroking fingers, igniting embers until fire burned in her belly and spread throughout her limbs.

"Faster, harder, deeper," he said, his breath coming in short, hard pants, much like her own. She leaned forward, the tips of her breasts brushing against the sleek satin comforter, the movement opening her to him even more so she could take him completely inside. He obliged her silent demand, carrying her dangerously close to the point of no return.

"Oo-oh," she whimpered, rocking hard against his hand as he continued to fill her. "Nolan," she cried, so close to the brink she teetered on the edge, reaching… "Nolan, please…"

She thrust her bottom higher, straining to take more, needing more, wanting more of him, but he withdrew his hand. Every cell in her body screamed in protest, but before she could voice her objection, he flipped her onto the bed, suspending her bottom over the edge of the mattress and looping her ankles over his shoulders.

Her back arched off the bed the moment his teeth lightly grazed her clit.

The sound that ripped from her chest sounded wild and so primitive the intensity of it frightened her. Her hips bucked, but he tightened his grip on her bottom and held her to him as he slowly made love to her with his mouth.

She didn't know how much more of the sensual onslaught she could stand, but he pushed her higher, then took her to a place she'd all but forgotten existed, a place where her defenses shattered, leaving her with nothing to shield herself from him.

With Nolan, only with him, did she welcome the relinquishment of her iron-fisted control. It had been too long since she'd been given the gift of reveling in the power it gave her to once again experience the vulnerability she'd otherwise never allow herself to feel. They were sexual equals, yet she never felt threatened by his dominance of her when they made love this way.

He drove her until she could no longer think, until she could barely catch her breath. His mouth. His hands. He tasted, stroked, laved and forced every erogenous zone into sharp contrast until her body became electrified with sensation.

He quickened the pace and she fisted her hands into the comforter, straining toward blessed fulfillment. Except he refused her. Now in complete control of her, he withheld what she so desperately needed. He slowed the pace again, carefully bringing her closer to earth, but before her feet came near the ground, he sent her soaring even higher than the last time.

The pressure inside her built hard and fast. Her stomach muscles ached. Her legs trembled. Her body felt weak, as if she no longer had the strength to go on, yet she still reached for the release her body was demanding.

She tried to pull him to her and her nails raked across his shoulder. He refused to relinquish the control she gave over to him, driving her harder, higher and faster one final time to the edge, holding her suspended until her begging cries for release segued into long, earthy moans of sublime ecstasy.

Wave after wave of pleasure cascaded over her, so exquisite her throat tightened and she had to squeeze her eyes shut to keep from weeping. He shifted her more fully onto the bed, then she felt him above her. She welcomed the long-awaited weight of his body moving over hers and she wrapped her legs around his waist, lifting her hips to meet his as he buried himself inside her.

She clung to him, absorbing the musky scents and erotic sounds of their lovemaking. He kept his promise to her, loving her with slow strokes. Sliding his hands beneath her bottom, he angled her, then pumped his hips, harder, faster, each thrust long and deep until he ground his pelvis against hers, his big body trembling above her with the incredible force of his own release.

His heart pounded against her breast and she held him to her, slowly smoothing her hands over the sculpted landscape of his back, slick from exertion. His weight pressed her into the mattress, so she placed soft, tender kisses against the side of his neck, which had been her code that he was squishing her.

"Give me…" he rasped, struggling to catch his breath, "…a second."

She could hardly breathe, so she poked him in the ribs with her finger. He grunted, but rolled off her.

"Still a pushy broad," he said with a chuckle. He hauled her up against his side and tucked her close.

She wiggled to find a comfortable position. He muttered something her exhausted mind refused to decipher as she nestled her head against his shoulder and tangled her legs with his. The sound of his breathing lengthened as he drifted off to sleep. She wasn't far behind, and as she closed her eyes, her last thought was of how glad she was that some things never changed.

10

NOLAN AWOKE EARLY Sunday morning with Mikki sprawled halfway across his chest. He tightened his hold on her and she murmured a protest in her sleep and hooked her hand over his shoulder, refusing to budge. She didn't need to worry. He wasn't about to let her go, now or ever.

They'd be returning to Frisco in a matter of hours, and he had yet to broach the subject of her drinking, which had spurred his spontaneous drive to Napa late Friday night. He supposed avoidance played a role to a certain degree since he didn't exactly look forward to confronting her, any more than he did the argument sure to follow. There been a time when he would've dodged the inevitable completely, but he wasn't the same guy that had once run at the first sign of trouble.

He wanted Mikki, for the long haul, and that made all the difference to him. The only reason he'd put off confronting her was that she'd created one hell of a distraction. When she'd walked out of the bathroom in nothing but a filmy excuse for a nightgown, one thought had been on his mind—making love to his wife.

He swept his hands down her back to her cute, rounded ass and felt the first stirring of arousal. They'd only come up for air a couple of times since Friday night, driven from the elegant suite in search of sustenance. They'd taken a stroll though a couple of the shops in the downtown village late yesterday morning, grabbed a bite to eat at one of the restaurants, then hurried back to their room to make love again until they'd gone out for a late supper.

As if by unspoken agreement, they'd steered clear of the hot topic of their divorce. They'd talked about their work, relevant court decisions, her family and some of the more disturbing current events and their conversations remained firmly grounded in neutral territory. For the most part, however, the weekend had been spent taking and giving each other pleasure.

The familiarity of her body enthralled him, as did the rediscovery of the dips and swells of her lush curves. Her uninhibited response to his touch drove him even more insane with desire than he remembered. There was a newness to her daring, a touch of wildness that had taken him by surprise but which he'd fully enjoyed. But the one aspect of their lovemaking that hadn't changed was the way she gave all of herself to him, to his lust-filled demands, allowing him to lead her on a journey of erotic discoveries, trusting him.

He frowned. If she could only trust him like that out of bed, he thought, his life would be a whole lot easier.

He rolled her onto to her back, then rested on his elbow beside her. Tugging down the sheet down, he watched her lift her arms over her head and stretch languidly. His dick was hard before she opened her eyes.

She smiled sleepily at him. "Good morning," she murmured, followed by a throaty "Hmm," when he lazily smoothed his hand over her abdomen. "A very good morning."

His fingers sifted through the dark thatch of curls. With her arms still above her head, she parted her legs and encouraged a more intimate exploration with an enticing roll of her hips. He took his sweet time, massaging her inner thighs, smoothing his hands over her hips and across her abdomen, along the deep curve of her waist and beneath the underside of her full, ample breasts. She moaned softly when he lightly teased her nipples into tight buds, then made an initial sound of protest as he reversed the path. He dragged his fingers through the springy curls growing more and more damp as her arousal peaked. He built her anticipation slowly and at great expense to his own limited control where she was concerned. The sight of her writhing beneath his hands, combined with the exotic sounds of her groans growing louder, was worth the price though.

Out of sheer frustration, she reached for his hand. He caught her wrist. "No, you don't," he said. "This is my fantasy." As he settled her hands above her head, the blue of her eyes darkened to the color of rich sapphire.

"I'm gonna make you pay." Her sexy threat was provocative, husky and filled with sinful promise.

He rose up and leaned over her. "Sure you will," he taunted, then kissed her long and slow. He took his time and pushed her as close to the edge as he could without giving in to her demands. He didn't know how much more he could take.

She fired his blood like no one else could, and she took a great deal of pleasure in teasing him. "You think I'm kidding?" she challenged in a breathy whisper as he laved a path to the slope of her breast.

"Bring it on," he dared her. He flicked his tongue over her nipple.

Her back arched and she let out a slow, sexy hiss of breath when his mouth closed over the rosy peak. A keening moan of pure delight followed.

She nudged his groin with her knee. "Touch me, Nolan," she whispered.

He suckled more deeply on her breast.

"Touch me. I'm wet. And so hot. I want you to touch me."

She kept her arms above her head on the pillow where he'd placed them. Her hips rolled and she bent her knees, parting her legs wider. Her hip brushed against his cock. "Hmm," she murmured. "So ready."

He was ready to explode.

The huskiness of her voice and the sexy, teasing taunts stirred his imagination. He lifted his head and looked at her, her slightly parted lips, her eyes simmering with heat. "Nice try, babe," he said, struggling for control.

A wicked smile curved her lush mouth. "Taste me, Nolan," she whispered. "Make me come with your tongue." She dragged her tongue across her bottom lip.

"Put your fingers inside me and suck my clit until I come on your tongue. Do it."

His heart all but stopped beating. His cock, wedged against the silky smooth skin of her hip, thickened and throbbed painfully.

She didn't touch him. She didn't need to. The images her words conjured were more than enough to push him to the limit and beyond.

He almost wished he hadn't started this game with her. Somewhere along the way she'd gained the upper hand, and it was killing him.

She pursed her lips into a sultry pout. "Poor baby." She shifted slightly and wiggled her backside against his erection. He nearly came out of his skin.

"So hard." She pulled that tongue-over-her-lip thing again and kept rubbing her bottom against him. "Let me kiss it. I'll make it even harder," she purred.

He let loose with a growl of frustration.

Her sultry laughter taunted him. "I warned you," she said, looking smug. "You should know better."

He rose up and moved over her. He wasn't about to surrender. There were two of them in his game and he never had been a gracious loser. "You'll have to do better than that," he said. "Now I'll have to make you beg."

Her eyes widened in surprise when he rolled off the mattress, took hold of her hips and pulled her to the edge of the bed. He snagged the pillows and arranged them beneath the small of her back, elevating her hips.

"Nolan?"

He fell to his knees in front of her and breathed in

the musky scent of her arousal. Her feminine flesh glistened. Struggling to hold on to that final thread of his sanity took supreme effort, and he wasn't making any guarantees on how long he could hold back.

He nudged her thighs wider, making her vulnerable. "Look at me, Mikki," he demanded, his voice hoarse. He pressed her folds open and exposed her core, then dipped his head and tongued her wet heat.

He'd angled her so she could watch him as he laved her, and he held her prisoner with his gaze. He wanted her to see the pleasure she gave him. Wanted her to watch as he made love to her so intimately. He teased her with his hands, drove her close to madness with his mouth until she was pleading with him for release. When he refused her, she swore at him in between pants of breath and groans of pleasure. Still, he refused, held her suspended on the brink until his control finally shattered, turning loose a primitive need to make her completely his.

He rose up and urged her onto her knees. She kicked the pillows aside and turned, pressing her sweet ass against his groin. Taking her hips in a firm grasp, he thrust into her slick, wet heat. She stiffened for the briefest moment, then lifted her backside higher and took all of him inside her.

She'd pushed him too far, beyond reason, beyond anything but the primal need to possess. Her cries of pleasure grew louder, the wildness of their lovemaking more heated, more demanding. She tightened and clenched his thick shaft, milking his cock with each deep stroke until they succumbed to the sheer bliss of release.

The sound of their ragged breathing registered first as the world slowly righted itself. He pulled Mikki to him and she turned in his arms and sagged against him. "I hope you can afford another night," she said in a breathless whisper. "I don't think I can walk, let alone drive back to the city."

Once feeling returned to his legs, he moved onto the bed with her and they collapsed on the mattress. With her close to his side, he found one of the pillows while she groped for the sheet to cover their sweat-soaked bodies. "Done," he said, still trying to catch his breath. "Let's make it a week."

She snuggled closer. "I wish."

So did he.

She giggled suddenly. "I remember when we thought a night at Motel 6 and dinner at McDonald's was a treat. Better be careful," she said. "I could get used to this."

"Then why don't you?" he said easily. Too easily, but he knew what he wanted and he pushed his luck. "Move in with me."

Despite the casualness of his tone, she tensed in his arms. "That's not a good idea."

A definite chill filled the air around them. If he was going to kill the buzz, he might as well go all the way.

"You know," he said, keeping his tone even, "there's been something I've been meaning to ask you."

"Let's not do this."

He brushed his hand over her hip, then traced lazy circles with this thumb. She still didn't relax.

"Just one question."

She expelled an impatient breath. "Just one."

He tucked his hand beneath her chin and tipped her head back to gauge her reaction. Caution, and even a trace of fear, lined her big blue eyes. "When exactly did you plan on telling me you're a recovering alcoholic?"

NOTHING RUINED a great weekend faster than reality, Mikki thought, and theirs had just gone down in flames. She gave the sash of the plush white courtesy robe a hard tug and dropped into one of the Queen Anne chairs in the sitting area of the suite.

Nolan emerged from the bathroom, showered and freshly shaved, looking gorgeous as usual. He wore a pair of black trousers and a charcoal crewneck sweater she suspected was cashmere. He'd gone from discount cheap when they'd been married to designer expensive, and the sleek look suited him to perfection.

His new and improved shopping habits were the least of her concerns. First, she had to find a way to get her keys away from him.

Never one to be slow on the uptake, he'd figured out he'd stunned her into a state of shock. Her staring at him with her mouth hanging open like a gaping fish had been a pretty big clue. He'd said they'd talk later, then coolly suggested *she* take a shower. She'd fallen for that one, all right. Not only had he stolen her keys off the dresser, he'd taken them with him into the bathroom and locked the door so she couldn't steal them back and leave.

Which was exactly what she'd been planning.

She crossed her legs and folded her arms over her knee, watching him as he sat on the edge of the bed and pulled on his socks and slipped his feet into a pair of casual loafers. Probably Gucci, she thought, and not on sale at the outlet mall, either.

She hated this feeling, hated it, hated it, hated it. Cornered, trapped. Imprisoned. Not being the one calling the shots. This was why she didn't do well in therapy, her inability to let someone else take charge for so much as a second.

She glared at him. They weren't screwing each other's brains out now. He *knew* she needed to be in control of her little corner of life, so why was he doing this to her? To intentionally keep her off balance, no doubt.

"I want my keys back."

He dropped his shaving kit into his black leather weekender bag. "Don't worry," he said. "They're in a safe place." He gave his pocket a pat.

After he zipped up his bag and set it on the floor of the closet, he joined her in the sitting area. He sat across from her and propped his ankle over his knee, then slung his arm along the scalloped back of the velvet love seat.

The epitome of casual elegance, she thought sarcastically. She wasn't being fair or logical, but it beat dealing with the reality he was going to bully her into facing. Just who did he think he was, anyway? What she did with her life was her business. She'd repossessed his interest the night she'd thrown him out.

"Who told you?" she asked sharply. "Which one of my sisters did you wear down? Rory? Or was it Lauren?" Lauren had always had one of those big-brother type crushes on Nolan.

"Neither," he said, his voice calm.

She narrowed her eyes. "I know Emma wouldn't tell you. She'd go off on some mystic-psychic-metaphysical spiel, which once you figured out the translation would mean if you had questions, go to the source."

"Which I think I just did," he reminded her. His brown eyes were patient. Which meant he'd wait her out if it took a month.

She chewed her thumbnail and looked away. He claimed he'd changed, and he honestly had, she realized. Only once had he purposely confronted her, and look that how that ended. In divorce. He no longer avoided the tough issues, but was determined to face them.

"I found out because the firm had you investigated," he finally said.

She frowned. "Me? Why?"

"Once the information about the divorce being invalid came out, the founding partners felt it was necessary to protect their interests."

Huh? What was she missing? "What are you talking about?"

"I have a fiduciary responsibility to the other partners, Mikki," he explained. "Since our divorce was never legal and we had no prenuptial agreement, you're entitled to half my assets. Any decent divorce attorney would argue that includes my interest in Turner, Crawford and Lowe."

"And a smarter attorney would argue assets gained after the marriage ended, despite the technicality that voided our divorce, were exempt from community property." She lifted her hand to stop his counter argument before he started. "Wait a minute. You're a partner? You actually made partner?"

A wry grin touched his mouth. "That surprises you?"

"Actually, yes. The man I was married to couldn't manage to keep a running total in his own checkbook, let alone manage a law firm." She gave him a hard look. "And for the record, I don't want your money. I never have."

"I know you don't."

"Good," she snapped.

The patience he'd exhibited thus far vanished all of a sudden. A deep frown lined his forehead and a hardness entered his eyes. "Were you busted for driving while intoxicated?"

The accusation in his voice felt like a slap and she looked away in shame.

"Do you have any idea how lucky you were?"

"I know." She kept her gaze averted, preferring the pattern of the Oriental rug to the disappointment or disgust or whatever was in his eyes that she couldn't bear to see. "I could've been disbarred if I hadn't been able to plead it down. I paid a big fine and agreed to rehab."

"Screw your career," he snapped. "You could've killed someone."

She looked up at him. "I know."

He dragged his hand through his hair. "What the hell were you thinking?"

"I wasn't," she admitted quietly, and lowered her gaze. She bit the inside of her lip and stared at the floor again.

He came off the sofa and crouched in front of her. He placed his finger beneath her chin, forcing her to look at him. "Why, Mikki?" he asked, his expression filled with concern. "How did this happen?"

A lump the size of a shot glass lodged in her throat. "It's complicated."

"Tell me."

She hadn't ever wanted him to find out she was an alcoholic. She'd struggled to keep it a secret during their marriage and had managed to keep her drinking under control for the most part. The times she had drank, though, had usually been excessive, but she'd been able to go weeks, sometimes months without giving in to the overwhelming desire for alcohol. But Nolan wasn't dumb. She knew he'd eventually put it all together and figure out she'd had a meltdown. Their separation had devastated her. She'd felt as if her world was ending the night he'd left, and even though she'd intentionally pushed him away, it hadn't hurt her any less. She'd needed something, anything, to numb her from the horrific pain tearing her up inside. If she'd only been a little stronger, if she'd only had a little more courage, she might have been able to give him what he'd wanted.

But she hadn't been that strong. She'd been terrified of telling him she'd not only lied to him about her past, but that he'd turn away from her in revulsion if he knew the things her father had done to her. But her fear had ended up costing her the one thing she hadn't been able to bear losing, anyway—the love of her life. She'd dug a bottle of bourbon out of the cupboard and, a plastic tumbler later, the pain had stopped and she'd kept it at bay until she gotten busted for drunk driving almost a year later.

She let out a sigh. "I'm an addict, Nolan. Addicts don't need a reason to drink or to shoot up or to swallow a few prescription drugs. It happens, and once we start, we don't have the willpower to stop."

"Addiction isn't about strength or willpower. Alcoholism is a disease."

"Been reading the literature, have you?"

"Mikki—"

"Look," she said and stood. "I appreciate the concern and all, but this really is *my* problem. I'm handling it. I admit I did have a setback recently, but I'm nine days sober, attending meetings and getting through it." A wry grin touched her mouth. "One day at a time," she said with only a mild inflection of sarcasm.

He straightened. "I'm concerned because I care about you." His hands settled on her shoulders. "I love you, Mikki. I care what happens to you."

"I love you, too." The admission slipped out so easily it took her completely by surprise. In the end, what did it matter? "But that doesn't change anything." She laughed, the sound cold and intentionally bitter. "Love isn't some miracle cure, Nolan. Three little words don't alter the fact that I'm still a drunk."

He winced at her sharply spoken words. "Don't say that."

"Why not? It's true." She shrugged out of his grasp. "The first step to recovery is admitting your addiction. I'm a drunk, Nolan. An alcoholic. A goddamned addict. Say it," she demanded hotly. "Let me hear you say, 'my wife is a drunk.'"

"Stop it, Mikki."

He looked ready to strangle her, but she was fighting for her survival even if he didn't realize what the battle was all about. "Come on, Nolan. It's only a disease, right? Say, 'my wife is drunk.'"

His eyes turned glacial. His expression could've been carved from granite. "Knock if off," he warned.

A smarter woman than her would've heeded that advice. One fighting for her life didn't have that luxury. If she walked away, he'd only follow her. And if she didn't push him hard enough, he'd never stay away from her. They could be happy—for a while. The last two days together proved that much to her, but he'd start with that itch to populate the earth with gorgeous little brown-haired, brown-eyed replicas of himself. Eventually he'd leave when she refused to be swayed by his arguments. And then where would she be? He might have fooled her once today, but that didn't mean she was dumb enough to believe for a minute she'd ever survive the aftermath of Nolan a second time.

"No, you knock it off and shove your sanctimonious bullshit," she said. They stood expensive loafer to lipstick-red toenails and she got in his face. "You think there's a difference between me and the junkie with a needle in his arm? What *disease* separates me from the drunks passed out on the picnic tables in Victorian Park? Well, let me be the one to inform you—not a goddamned thing."

"You have people who love you, Mikki. Your family. Me." He lowered his voice and let out a rough sigh. He scrubbed his hand down his face. "We're all here to help you."

She shrugged carelessly. "Who says the boys in the park don't?"

"You can't help someone who isn't willing to help themselves."

"And you can't help someone who doesn't want your help, either," she countered.

His expression suddenly turned curious. He stared at her, hard, as if he might see all the way to her soul, all the way to her secrets, if he looked close enough.

He made her nervous as hell.

"That was a hint, by the way." She turned and started to walk away, but he grabbed her by the wrist.

"I'm on to you."

She shot him a frosty glare, then forced a sudden smile. "I'd rather have you in me." She looked him up and down. "Whaddya say? One for the road?"

He didn't so much as flinch. "I fell for your game once. Give it up, Mikki. It doesn't work on me anymore."

Her gaze dipped to his fly. "Pity."

"You're trying hard to push me away. Why? What am I getting too close to?" He narrowed the distance between them. "What are you so afraid of?"

He crowded her, invaded her comfort zone. She didn't like it. "Not you, that's for damned sure." She was terrified of him because she'd never be able to crawl back from under rock bottom the next time.

"No, you're not afraid of me," he said, "You're afraid I'll see too much of you."

She tried to tug free.

He tightened his hold.

"Go to hell." She spat the words at him. "And take your armchair psychology with you." Why wouldn't he leave her alone? He should be out the door by now, but she had a sinking feeling her standard operating procedure had seriously backfired on her.

"I've already been to hell and back. Not my idea of fun."

"Break open the bourbon, babe. I'll show you some real fun."

"What's your trigger, Mikki?" He pushed her now, and she didn't like having the tables turned on her. "What sends you reaching for that shot of bourbon?"

"Not a shot, a bottle."

"That would explain the hangover last weekend. What did it?"

He grabbed hold of her other wrist and held her prisoner. "What excuse did you sell yourself so you could dive headfirst into a shot glass?"

She would've slapped him, but he'd outsmarted her. Again. Stupid, the man wasn't.

He hauled her up against him and held her to him. She wiggled, she pushed, she tried every move she could think of to be free of him, but he refused to let her go. His arms were like steel bands around her, holding her captive, forcing her to face more than the truth, but her fear.

Tears burned her eyes. She tried to blink them away, but she lost the battle. The fight went out of her and she sagged against him, too emotionally exhausted to keep up the pretense any longer, but still not brave enough to be one-hundred percent honest with him.

"What set you off again, Mikki?" he asked her, gentling his tone and loosening his hold on her. "What is it you're so afraid to face?"

She pulled away from him and he let her go. She wiped the tears away with the heel of her hand. "Myself," she admitted, knowing he wouldn't back down or leave her alone until he got the truth out of her. She pulled in a shaky breath. "If I'm numb, then I can't hurt."

"What hurts?" He brushed away a tear with the pad of his thumb. "Tell me, Mikki," he demanded gently.

If only she could, but she didn't have the much courage. She opted for a fraction of the truth instead. "You, Nolan," she told him. "Loving you hurts like hell."

11

"YOU'VE CHANGED THE recipe, haven't you?" Mikki wrinkled her nose and returned the half-eaten chocolate éclair to the rose-patterned china desert plate.

Rory glanced up from the balls of dough she was forming. "Nope." She dropped three dough balls into the round cup of a muffin tin. "Same recipe."

"Maybe the chocolate went bad." Mikki got up from the stool at the butcher-block worktable and walked to the coffee urn for another refill. "Did you taste it first?"

"There's nothing wrong with the chocolate." Rory cast her a sideways glance. "The coffee apparently meets your approval," she added in a lightly chastising tone. "That's your third cup this morning."

"Fifth," Mikki corrected, then took a tentative sip. "I had two before I left the apartment." Tucking her hand into the front pocket of her black twill slacks, she rested her backside against the stainless counter. "Late night."

A bad night, actually. One of her worst in that she'd come dangerously close to succumbing to the gnawing pangs that had driven her from her apartment in a reckless search for a bar where no one knew her. Thankfully she'd come to her senses before throwing away her latest round of sobriety. She'd ended up in an all-night diner near the interstate, trading baseball trivia and football stats with a pair of truckers over banana cream pie and coffee until three in the morning.

What's your trigger, Mikki?

Wishful thinking, she thought. And enough regret to fill an ice hockey rink.

The uncontrollable desire for a drink had been exacerbated by a tug-on-the-ol'-heartstrings cell phone commercial between the fifth and sixth innings of the Oakland A's game. The ad had shown two older couples each waiting for the news that they were officially grandparents. One couple waited by the telephone, going to extreme measures not to miss the call, while the cell phone couple were having the time of their lives dining and dancing the night away.

Where were all the acid reflux ads or goofy dancing hamster video store commercials when a girl really needed them? She hadn't wanted to think about babies or parents waiting to become grandparents. She'd made her decision and it didn't matter that she'd never be the one with parents and in-laws waiting for the arrival of the next generation. She'd made her choices.

What's your trigger, Mikki?

"Stupidity," she muttered in self-disgust. She couldn't blame the product-hawkers for her near slip last night. Or Nolan, for that matter.

Don't forget guilt, her conscience reminded her.

How could she? It was her constant companion lately.

Her issues with booze were hers. Period. She was the one who sought out an easy, mind-numbing cure because she'd let down her guard and allowed a weak moment of sadness, painful memories, loneliness or stupid daydreams for things she knew weren't her destiny.

She pushed off the counter, walking back to the table, pretending not to notice Rory's curious glance. Her sister continued to form more balls of dough. Why she did so when she had a more than capable staff to do it for her was beyond Mikki.

She slid the plate with the half-eaten éclair close, then shoved it away again. "You sure that chocolate isn't bad? If Lauren wouldn't eat them, something must be wrong."

Her mom and younger sister had been at Lavender Field earlier for breakfast, but because she'd been running late, Mikki had missed them by a good thirty minutes. Just as well, she figured, considering her current mood.

"I'm sure." Rory blew out a puff of breath to move a loose strand of dark hair from her eyes. "Besides, what's wrong with Lauren isn't related to food," she said. The hair fluttered back into her line of vision and she used the back of her hand to push it away, leaving a smudge of flour on her forehead.

"Oh?" Mikki prompted, relieved to have something to think about other than her own sorry life.

"Josh called while she and Mom were here," Rory explained. "She was upset afterward and tried to play it cool, but you know how easy it is read Lauren."

Mikki dragged her finger through the rich chocolate covering the éclair. "I'll call her this afternoon and make sure she's okay. Maybe she'll be ready to talk by then."

She tasted the chocolate again. "It's—" she sucked the last of the gooey confection from her finger "—I dunno. Off."

"Maybe it's you who's off," Rory suggested. She dropped three more dough balls into the muffin tin. "Something happen in Napa you want to talk about?"

"Not especially." She shot for a cheery tone, but Rory's you're-so-full-of-it glance told her she hadn't even come close. She really hated to burden her sister when she had enough on her pastry sheet with the added stress over the design and construction of her fourth store under way, but since Rory knew she'd spent the weekend with Nolan, she'd been expecting an interrogation.

She cradled the mug in her hands, toying with the handle. "He knows," she blurted, feeling relieved and six kinds of miserable all at the same time.

Rory dusted flour from her hands, her expression skeptical. "You told him?"

Mikki blew out a stream of breath. "What do you think?"

While Rory poured herself a cup of coffee, Mikki explained how Nolan had confronted her about being a recovering alcoholic. "And I was my usual charming self, of course," she admitted miserably. "He's probably waiting for the clerk's office to open as we speak so he can file for divorce himself."

Rory pushed the hair from her eyes again. Propping her hip against the butcher-block table, she studied Mikki over the rim of her cup. "I thought you wanted the divorce?"

Mikki wasn't fooled by her sister's nonchalance. She knew a serious inquisition coming when she saw one. "I do."

Rory's arched brows arched higher. "Do you?" she asked, suspicion personified.

The problem with having someone know you so well was that they did. "Okay, fine," she said with a frown. "So we had a spectacular weekend and didn't argue once until he had to go and ruin it by dragging reality into the suite with us." Her frown deepened. "But up until then, it was just sex."

Rory's expression went from suspicious to give-me-a-break disbelief.

Mikki squirmed. She drained the last of her coffee and considered another cup, even though her stomach had started protesting two cups ago. "*Nothing* has changed," she stated emphatically. "The reason we separated in the first place won't, either, and you know it."

"Meaning you still refuse to consider the possibility of starting a family."

"Precisely."

"And of course you finally explained to him why you feel that way, right?"

Guilt hit Mikki hard and she looked away. There were a lot of things she could face, but telling Nolan why she wouldn't ever have a child was not going to be one of them anytime soon.

"I thought so." Rory set her mug on the table with a thump. "Well, then, congratulations. You have everything just the way you want it."

"It really is better this way." Mikki wondered which of them she was attempting to convince. Nolan had already suggested she move in with him. Not that she planned to take him up on that offer, but if she did, it wouldn't be much longer before he'd be at her again to start a family. It was no mystery how that would end.

No, they really were better off apart. He needed to move on, to find himself a woman who wanted children as much as he did. In twenty-five years or so, he and the missus could wine and dine all night long with the cell phone nearby as they waited to hear the news about the birth of their first grandchild, too, for all she cared.

What's your trigger, Mikki?

She needed a drink. Bad.

Rory shrugged. "If you say so."

"I do," Mikki snapped, more irritated by the gut-clenching desire for two finger's worth of bourbon than Rory's dismissive attitude.

Straight up. And keep them coming, dammit.

"Nolan doesn't need to know—any of it," she added in a fierce whisper. "And he won't. *Ever.*" She tried to take a breath, but it was as if the air had suddenly been sucked out of the room.

She would've let the swearing rip if she could breathe. Instead, she hopped off the stool and stalked away. She dragged open the heavy metal door, pushed on the screen and slipped into the back alley. She had to get a grip. That same sense of claustrophobia she'd felt after the stupid commercial made her cry last night returned, draining her already-depleted energy levels. She felt just as hemmed in, just as trapped as she had last night, and she didn't have a clue how to make the feeling go away without a drink.

Bracing her hands against the rough, red brick wall of the building, she dropped her head forward and concentrated on taking in small amounts of air. She loved her sisters and would crawl over broken glass for them, but Rory was asking too much of her. How could she possibly tell Nolan the reason she didn't want children was that she was terrified of what she might do to them?

She'd already proven she had zero willpower where he was concerned. What if he broke past the one barrier she'd managed to keep erected and she did get pregnant? She could not, would not, take that chance. A Correlli had no business having babies. It was a fact of life, and a prophecy she had no interest in fulfilling. The cycle stopped with her.

"Screw that," she muttered. She fisted her hands, scraping her knuckles on the brick. No way was she going to subject a kid to one ounce of the hell she'd suffered.

Mikki looked up when the screen door squeaked. "I'm fine," she told Rory.

"Are you sure?"

The concern in Rory's eyes heaped another serving

of guilt on Mikki's shoulders. She pushed off the wall and started to pace the narrow length of concrete slab. "Just freaking peachy."

She shoved her hands into the pockets of her slacks and looked at Rory. Her sister was one of the most gentle, loving people she knew and didn't deserve to be her whipping post. "I'm sorry," she said, tempering her tone. "Don't worry. I'll be fine. But jeez, Rory, you of all people—"

"Mikki." Rory stopped her with a hand on her arm. "Nolan loves you. Really loves you. That won't change if you tell him what your father did to you."

"You don't know that," Mikki argued. Dammit, she knew differently. Experience had taught her that lesson. Not even love could conquer revulsion.

"Mikki—"

"No. I can't do this now," she said, pulling away. "I have to go." She brushed past Rory and returned to the workroom. She found her purse and briefcase with her sweater near the table where she'd left them.

"Don't you ever get tired of running?" One corner of Rory's mouth quirked, suggesting that she was aware she'd practiced her own version of denial since the deep pain of her own failed engagement.

"I'm not running." She came off defensive, but had slipped way past the point of caring. Only self-preservation mattered now. It's all that ever really mattered, she thought, and wondered if she'd ever truly get past all the garbage.

"I need—" *a drink* "—to meet a client." There were

bars open before nine in the morning in San Francisco, and she knew just where to find them.

She knew where to find an AA meeting, too. But a few drinks would be so much more comforting.

Numbing.

Rory crossed her arms and gave her a level stare, her gentle green eyes uncharacteristically hard. "I understand why you *think* you shouldn't have children. I happen to disagree, but that's not what this is really about, is it?"

Mikki shoved her arms through the sleeves of her black cotton cardigan and yanked it into place. "I don't know what you're talking about," she lied, adjusting the sleeves with a couple of sharp tugs. She knew what Rory wanted from her, but that was one wager she couldn't afford to place. She'd rather Nolan go on believing she was a selfish bitch than risk seeing his beautiful dark eyes fill with contempt—for her.

"Yes, you do," Rory countered in a calm voice that raised Mikki's hackles. "You're so afraid Nolan will be disgusted if he knows what happened to you."

"It's ancient history, Rory," she warned. And better left buried in the ruins of the past.

"But you'd rather push him away than face the truth. How long are you going to let something you had no control over keep you from being happy?"

Mikki opened her mouth to tell Rory where she could stick her Monday morning quarterbacking philosophy, but the dull ringing in Mikki's ears drowned out the words. Her hands trembled, followed by quaking in her knees. She reached behind her for the stool, then sat before she took a nosedive onto the floor at Rory's feet. Her physical reaction had nothing to do with too much coffee and not enough sleep, but the truth her sister had just shoved down her throat.

Denial was so much more comforting. And easier to digest. She'd been telling herself she was happier alone for such a long time that she actually believed the lie. But Rory was right, and choking down the truth was unsettling and difficult for her to admit. She feared Nolan would be repulsed by her almost as much as the healing process terrified her. Fears deeply rooted in harsh reality, supported by concrete evidence.

During her freshman year at Cal State Berkeley, she'd started having nightmares, brought on, she'd discovered, by the sudden changes and upheaval caused when she'd gone off to college. She wasn't sleeping, her grades were slipping and she was withdrawing from everyone around her, her family included. Emma had urged her to consider therapy, something she'd always refused, but she'd reluctantly taken her mom's advice.

She'd progressed slowly and the sessions always left her feeling drained, raw and exposed emotionally. Shoveling skeletons out of the closet wasn't easy for someone who'd been keeping secrets for more than a decade, but she couldn't argue with the effectiveness since the frequency of her nightmares had diminished. So she'd continued with the weekly sessions and eventually started feeling more like herself again.

By the start of her sophomore year her usual distrust

of men had lessened to the point where she'd even dated occasionally. When she'd met Clay Donovan, they'd become a couple almost immediately. He'd been sweet, funny, smart and, most importantly, she hadn't felt threatened or intimidated by him as she had with a lot of guys with more overbearing personalities.

Naturally, she'd discussed her blossoming relationship with her therapist, who'd begun to persuade her that revealing her past to Clay would be another step toward healing. If they were indeed serious about each other, then she needed to trust him with the truth.

"Trust." She spat out the word. Trust was nothing but a crock. What had it gotten her? Not a damned thing.

She'd trusted not only her therapist, but Clay's line of crap about his feelings for her, and she'd made a colossal error in judgment. He'd had been horrified by the things she'd told him and she had barely scratched the surface of the emotional and physical abuse she'd endured at her father's hands. Even more humiliating, he'd reacted as if *she* were the one responsible, then disappeared so fast, she'd nearly choked on the fumes from the vapor trail left in his wake.

Consciously she understood what she'd laid on a twenty-year-old guy was pretty heavy duty, but that hadn't prevented the hurt and shame from tearing her up inside. She didn't remember much beyond Clay dumping her that night because she'd gotten roaring drunk for the first time to block out the pain. Somehow, she ended up at Rory's apartment two days later. Her sister had sobered her up and she'd cried on Rory's shoulder for a week before finally summoning the courage to return to school.

She hadn't seen the inside of a therapist's office since. And she never again spoke of the abuse she'd survived—not even with her husband.

Rory went to the sink, pulled a glass from the shelf above and filled it with water. "Here," she said, setting the glass in front of Mikki. "Drink this."

"I can't tell him." Mikki stared at the glass until all the oxygenation drifted to the top of the water line and disappeared before lifting her gaze to Rory's. "I can't do it. Rory, what if he…" She closed her eyes. "I don't think I could handle it if he…"

"He won't," Rory reassured her.

Mikki clung to the firm conviction in her sister's voice, desperately wanting to believe her. Nolan *had* changed since their separation, and she clung to that small slice of hope, too. The man he'd been would have avoided the subject of her alcoholism like the plague, not force the issue out into the open the way he had yesterday. Granted, he'd always met her head-on, but now when she tried to push him away, he stubbornly refused to back down and kept returning for more.

"It's been twelve years since I talked about any of this," she told Rory. "I'm not sure I even know where to start."

Rory went back to her side of the butcher block and worked on finishing up the cloverleaf rolls. The hint of a smile curved her wide mouth. "Your strongest defense is always a stronger offense."

"Oh, for the…" Mikki shook her head and managed a small wry smile. "Gee, thanks a lot for the advice, *Mom*."

"That was one of yours, by the way."

"Oh." Mikki put her elbow on the table and rested her head against her palm. "It won't be easy, I hope you know."

"I know. But you're not alone, Mikki," Rory reminded her. "We'll always be here for you."

"Nolan said the same thing yesterday," Mikki said. "I hope he meant it."

"Has he ever lied to you?" Rory asked.

Mikki let out a weary sigh and traced lazy circles in the dusting of flour on the worktable. "No," she said. "That, he hasn't done."

"Then you have nothing worry about, do you?"

She shot Rory a get-real glance, but her sister's attention was occupied by setting the temperature gauge of the large, industrial oven. "I wish I had a crystal ball to let me know how this was going to turn out," she said as Rory walked back toward the table.

"Well," Rory said, her voice tinged with humor, "we could always consult Mom's tea leaves first."

Mikki reached for the chocolate éclair and finished it off in three bites. "You know," she said, licking a smear of chocolate from her fingers before shooting her sister a sly grin, "that was pretty good. You have changed the recipe, haven't you?"

BY THURSDAY AFTERNOON, Nolan had reached the limit of his patience. He hadn't heard a word from Mikki since Napa and was fed up with her silence. If he kept waiting for her to make a decision about their future, he'd be looking at retirement.

Enough was enough.

He reached for the phone and punched his assistant's three-digit extension into the keypad. "Ozzie," he barked into the receiver. "Anything?"

"My source in the clerk's office says nada," Ozzie replied, unfazed by Nolan's brusque manner. "No *Baylor vs. Baylor* on file today."

Nolan breathed a sigh of relief and hung up the phone. Since Monday he'd had Ozzie checking with the court clerk's office to see if Mikki had filed for divorce. Four days and nothing. That had to be a good sign. Yet, as much as it gave him hope, it filled him with an equal dose of frustration. Her silence tested the limits of his patience, but waiting to be served with a summons and complaint for divorce from a dispassionate process server was just damned annoying.

He'd wanted to give her time, but she'd had more than enough. Five years' worth, according to his calendar.

Inaction wasn't his style. He hadn't gained the record he had by waiting around for the other side to make the first move. He always struck the first blow, then advanced until the opposition caved under the pressure.

So why was he treating the situation with Mikki differently?

Because, he thought as he ran his hand through his

hair, he didn't know if she could hold up under the pressure. She wasn't opposing counsel, she was his wife. His alcoholic wife.

Loving you hurts like hell.

Her words had been haunting him all week and guilt had settled in his gut like a lead weight. He'd pushed her hard their last day in Napa. Maybe too hard. For all he knew she could be swimming in the bottom of a whiskey barrel, and he held himself responsible.

He strode to the window and looked down at the red and white lights from the sea of vehicles in rush-hour traffic creeping along the crowded boulevard twenty floors below his office. Was she out there? Sitting in traffic, trying to get home after a tough day, or would she be heading for the closest watering hole to drink herself into mind-numbing oblivion? He didn't like that he didn't know the answer any more than he liked to think of Mikki sitting on some bar stool, fending off tired pickup lines from a parade of jerks hoping to get lucky. Or maybe not, he thought, jealousy slicing through him.

Don't even go there.

He blew out a stream of breath. More hot air. That's all his big speech about being there for her had been—nothing but a big blast of hot, empty air. By giving her space, he hadn't done either of them any favors and only proved to her his word wasn't worth squat.

Give her space, my ass, he thought with a grunt of self-loathing. He'd been too busy following right in his old man's footsteps and distancing himself from the truth.

He'd changed, all right. He'd morphed right into the bastard he'd despised most of his life.

Nolan had just finished college when his mother had succumbed to her illness and taken her own life. He hadn't hesitated to blame his dad. His mom had needed her husband, but Trenton couldn't be bothered with an emotionally unstable wife.

After the funeral, Nolan had made sure the old man held no misconceptions about who he held accountable for his mother's suicide. From there, their argument had spiraled out of control. Nolan had called his dad an arrogant, self-absorbed prick and Trenton had remained true to form by threatening to cut his son out of his life.

Nolan had saved him the trouble.

Without his old man's support, he couldn't afford law school, so he'd gone to work in construction with Tucker. Because his dad was a state senator, the other tradesmen ribbed him, but he'd worked hard and eventually the rich kid had earned their respect.

Close to three years later he'd saved enough money to support himself through his first year of school, and he'd still struggled financially. At the start of his second year, he'd gone to pay his expenses for the semester and discovered his account had been paid in full.

A letter from his father's attorney informed him his education expenses would be paid from the proceeds of a trust that had belonged to his mother. Although he'd never found proof to the contrary, Nolan suspected the trust had been nothing more than a fabrication, his old man's way of attempting to make amends. He'd been tempted to refuse, but for once his common sense had overruled his pride. He'd taken the money for school under the guise in which it was offered, but had made it abundantly clear he'd accept nothing more.

His dad had made a few more gestures toward a reconciliation up until his death a couple of years ago, but Nolan never even tried to make an effort. In the end, his father had gotten in the last word by leaving everything he owned to his only son. Nolan had been on the verge of giving it all to charity but roots and family history were important to him and he still harbored the hope of one day passing it all on to his own children. Maybe he should've swallowed some of that Baylor pride.

Then why didn't you?

Because it hurt too much.

Nolan turned away from the window and walked back to his desk. No, he thought, he hadn't because his anger was easier to hold on to than admitting he could've been wrong.

Loving you hurts like hell.

Maybe his dad had loved his mom to the point he'd had no other choice but to withdraw. Maybe the pain of seeing the woman he'd loved slowly lose her grip on reality had been too much for him to bear.

Nolan blew out a heavy sigh. Maybe what his father had done had simply been a matter of survival.

Now there was a concept Nolan could grasp with both hands. Wasn't that exactly what he was doing? Keeping his distance from Mikki, not because he thought she needed space or time. Those were nothing more than convenient excuses. And sorry ones at that; in reality, distance was easier than admitting he could be partially responsible for sending her over the edge.

He rubbed at the knot of tension in his neck. He didn't regret forcing her to confront the issue of keeping her alcoholism from him, but he did regret pushing her the way he had because of the hurt he'd caused her. Hurt she'd tried to hide behind anger.

A self-deprecating grin twisted his mouth. She had been furious with him, vehemently fighting him. Ducking and running for cover hadn't been options when those blue eyes of hers had sizzled brightly with anger. There'd been no heading for the nearest exit this time, he thought, even when she'd laid into him with her viperous tongue. But they'd played that game before and she...

Had played him like a fool?

"Dammit," he muttered. What he'd learned the past week about alcoholism wouldn't fill a champagne flute, but he knew enough about his wife to know when she was trying to blow smoke up his ass. Why hadn't he seen it sooner?

For as much as Mikki rarely backed down from a fight, she also knew a few tricks when it came to dodging stray bullets. When the smart-ass sarcasm hadn't worked on him, she'd changed tactics. Full-blown temper hadn't fazed him, but he'd surrendered when she'd dragged out the most lethal weapon in any woman's arsenal—tears. The minute her eyes pooled up with a hint of moisture, he'd backed off fast, playing right into her devious little hands.

He was definitely out of practice, because he hadn't even realized what she'd done. The teary-eyed bit had never been Mikki's gig. So why had she felt she'd had to resort to turning on the water works? What the hell was she so afraid of?

What else was she hiding from him?

He honestly didn't have the first clue, but whatever had her running scared, he wasn't about to let her face it alone.

Ozzie walked into Nolan's office with a thick stack of documents and a grim expression. "These just came by courier," he said, setting them in front of Nolan. "A Motion to Lift Stay and a hearing notice for a temporary restraining order. Not so bad, right?"

A motion to lift the injunction on the Delaney adoption and a notice of hearing on a Temporary Restraining Order that would prevent his client from having any contact with the minor were no less than he would've done himself. "No, it's not so bad," Nolan said absently, giving the motion a cursory glance. He'd just have the T.R.O. quashed and immediately file that request for supervised visitation.

Ozzie cleared his throat and tapped his finger on the upper left corner of the motion's face sheet. "Have a familiar ring to it?"

Nolan read the name of the attorney the court had appointed Guardian ad Litem for Zoe Delaney. *Michaela Correlli.*

"Aw, hell."

Ozzie snickered. "I know what this is," he said.

"So do I," Nolan said. "A train wreck looking for a place to happen."

So much for his going on the offensive and advancing until the opposition caved under the pressure. Mikki had drawn first blood, and he suspected the battle would become nothing short of massacre.

12

SHOES, MIKKI THOUGHT, staring at the navy slide dangling from her big toe, weren't all they were cracked up to be. Regardless of the price tag, when one fell, the other was sure to drop soon after, or in her case, come back around to give her a good swift kick in the rear.

Waiting for the fall, or swift kick, wore on her nerves and was playing hell with her waistline. She'd consumed a package of stale chocolate-coated mini donuts she'd found in her desk and two caramel lattes from the coffeehouse across the street. A third was currently under consideration, and maybe a slice of that scrumptious-looking, raspberry-cream-cheese crumb cake.

In the two and one half hours since she'd had Nolan served with the motion to have the Stay on the Delaney adoption lifted and a Temporary Restraining Order preventing his client contact with Zoe, she'd heard zip, and probably gained five pounds. He had twenty days to file a reply brief, but she expected him to make some sort of retaliatory move on his client's behalf. At the very least she expected a phone call from him, if for no other reason than to give her a load of grief about not warning him she'd been appointed to the Delaney case.

With a flick of her toe, the other shoe landed on the gray industrial-grade carpeting near its mate. If only she could exert as much control over the rest of her life, maybe she wouldn't have made such a mess of things. Her relationship with Nolan, in particular.

She started to read the psychiatric evaluation performed by an independent therapist. Although the psychologist concluded Zoe could suffer a dramatic setback if she were removed from the Michaelsons' care, he also went on to state that preventing Zoe from establishing a bond with her biological mother could prove equally harmful to the girl's emotional development. The report continued to quote statistics from various sources in support of the conclusion. In essence, the report had been a waste of time and money.

Her job wasn't to appease either the Michaelsons or Amelia Ferguson, but to represent Zoe and to recommend to the court what was best for the girl. Returning her to her mother's custody, especially after the woman had abandoned her and left her in the care of her monstrous father, was not the answer. However, she also agreed with the therapist's findings that Zoe shouldn't be denied a relationship with her birth mother. Mikki knew from experience with other minors she'd represented, if the situation wasn't handled properly, Zoe could end up with any number of problems later in life.

After her visit to the Michaelson home late yesterday afternoon, her decision was even more difficult.

Maureen hadn't exaggerated, and Mikki agreed that Zoe was a bright, beautiful nine-year-old little girl who'd overcome incredible obstacles in her short life-span. Mikki had read the file and knew that when Zoe had first been placed in the Michaelsons' care there had been several behavioral problems to contend with. Mikki hadn't seen any indication of unresolved issues in that area.

As for Bobbie and John Michaelson, they were warm, kind and they showered Zoe with love and affection. They also had two other, biological children, a boy, twelve, and a girl, Zoe's age. In the few hours Mikki had spent observing the family, she understood why Zoe had managed to make the progress she had, and just how the Michaelsons deserved so much of the credit. She could pick any one of the minors she'd represented over the years from similar circumstances and she'd be hard pressed to find a handful who'd made the amazing progress Zoe had.

She dropped the report back on her desk, then eased back in her chair. With her calves propped on the file drawer of her desk atop the dark green Oakland A's pillow she kept hidden inside, she released a tired sigh. She'd been working late all week and should probably call it a night, but the thought of no one waiting for her when she got home made her feel even more alone.

She supposed she had no one to blame but herself. It wasn't as if she'd done anything to resolve all those loose dangling ends she despised. Rory was right. She was a wimp.

As he'd done all week long, Nolan continued to occupy her thoughts. She opened her eyes and looked at the phone, debating whether or not to call him, then decided against it. The conversation she needed to have with him was strictly reserved for a face-to-face meeting—regardless of the outcome.

Wimp.

Yup, she thought. Major wimp.

She stared hard at the phone, wondering where he was, what he was doing and why the hell he hadn't called her. She'd spent a good deal of time at the courthouse and she'd looked for him there each time, only to suffer equal shares of relief and disappointment when she hadn't seen him. She tortured herself with fantasies and memories of their lovemaking until her body ached with need. When she wasn't visualizing him hot and hard and naked, she was in a constant state of dread over what his reaction would be if she ever had the guts finally to be completely honest with him.

She'd considered dozens of methods of approach, but somehow had never managed to develop a sound strategy. Any conversation with a we-need-to-talk beginning was destined to end in disaster. She'd punched in his number countless times throughout the day and night, only to lose her nerve and hang up because she didn't know what to say.

Yesterday when she'd met her sisters for a quick lunch in between court appearances, Lauren had asked her if she still planned to file for divorce. She'd hesitated long enough to prompt a warning from Lauren that she wasn't being fair to Nolan. Her sister was right, but that didn't alleviate her irritation. She knew she wasn't doing either of them any favors by dragging out the inevitable, but something kept holding her back.

Hope?

Rory just out and called her a wimp, but for very different reasons. Another accusation she hadn't been able to deny.

She settled more deeply in the chair and closed her eyes again. She really should go home. The Oakland A's had the night off and were heading for home after two straight losses to the Yankees, but the San Francisco Giants were on the road in Cincinnati and their hot new rookie was scheduled to pitch tonight. Maybe she'd stop at Felucca's for takeout. An Italian sub, diet cola and the game didn't seem like such a bad idea. She did have a couple of cases still needing attention, but she could take them home with her.

Although, she thought with a slight quirk of her mouth, there were much more interesting ways to spend an evening than working. Making love to Nolan naturally being at the top of her list. If she hadn't turned into such a wuss, she might drive up to his place and fulfill that little fantasy.

Two more minutes, she thought and yawned. She'd pack it in, stop at Felucca's and head for home—alone.

Settling further back in her chair, she sucked in a deep breath and could practically smell the intoxicating blend of spices. She imagined hard salami, pepperoni and mortadella sprinkled with fresh peppers and roma tomatoes. Smother it all with melted provolone and mozzarella, add a dusting of freshly grated Parmesan, then warm olive oil and…citrus?

She opened her eyes. Her heart stuttered, then hammered heavily in her chest.

Nolan.

Damn, he looked good. Undeniably handsome in a relaxed sort of way that made him impossible for her to resist. He held the jacket of his charcoal suit in the crook of his finger, the designer fabric slung casually over his shoulder. He leaned against the doorjamb with a wicked grin on his face that filled her with anticipation. The sleeves of his white shirt with dove-gray pinstripes were rolled back, revealing the corded muscle of his forearms. Just the thought of all that strength and power holding her, keeping her safe, made her knees go weak.

He held up a white paper sack imprinted with the Felucca's Deli logo. Those mouthwatering forearms rippled. She loved a man who knew good deli.

His mouth slanted into a lopsided grin. "Free for dinner?"

Only if he promised to be dessert.

She straightened and stuffed the pillow back into its hiding place. "If you're here to give me lip about the motion," she said, closing the drawer, "save it for your reply brief." She tucked the psychiatric evaluation back into the file and moved the heavy folder to the corner of her desk.

A predatory gleam entered his gaze as he pushed off

the doorjamb. He strolled casually into her office, closing the door behind him. "That isn't why I'm here."

The sexy promise in his eyes, combined with the purposeful intent in his voice, sent her pulse rate careening straight into the danger zone. Hunger that nothing to do with food awakened in a flash, stirring her blood with anticipation. By the time he reached her side of the desk, her panties were drenched.

"Then why are you here?" She didn't much care if he had an ulterior motive, just so long as he fulfilled a fantasy or two.

He dropped the sack on her desk and reached for her. "I missed my wife," he said, and hauled her out of the chair and right into his arms.

Before she could issue her standard "ex" addendum, his mouth clamped over hers in a kiss so hot she considered it a miracle they didn't burst into flames. His hands smoothed over her back, glancing down her spine, running up her sides then back down again to her cup her bottom and pull her tight against him.

Oh, God, I've missed you, too.

She sank her fingers into his thick, silky hair and moved against him, brushing against the wide, hard expanse of his chest. Her breasts tingled and swelled, her nipples beading into tight, sensitive peaks. She ached for his touch, for the feel his large, warm hands cupping her, for the velvety softness of his tongue suckling her, pulling her into his mouth.

She'd left far too many loose ends between them, and just as she'd feared would happen, the proverbial big fat noose had indeed been slipped over her neck and pulled a little tighter with each passing day. There was so much she wanted to say to him, things he needed to know, but she didn't have a clue how or where to begin, or even what she hoped to accomplish.

She felt as if she were standing on a faulty trap door with the latch ready to give way. Any minute now, she'd swing.

Compounding her mistakes, she buried the uncertainty of the future for the immediacy of simply being in her husband's arms. Freeing her mind of everything but the steady rush of heat pulsating in her veins, she welcomed the sharp need tugging low in her belly. For once, she didn't stop to question the inevitable, but reached for the moment and refused to relinquish her hold.

Her senses vibrated with every sound, every touch. The rustle of fabric, their ragged breathing. Nolan's hands on her bottom, lifting her onto the edge of her desk. The rattle of her chair being shoved aside. The urgency of their hands—his removing her panties, hers tugging down his zipper to free him from the confines of his trousers and briefs.

She didn't waste energy on worry or fear, only on answering the mutual demands of their bodies. He scooted her bottom closer to the edge of the desk, parted her legs, then separated her folds to slowly ease his fingers inside her. Exquisite sensation exploded. Her hand tightened around his shaft, growing even more impossibly thick as she mimicked the long, slow thrusts of his fingers.

Their gazes locked. Tension coiled tight. She bit down hard on her lip to keep from crying out so they wouldn't be discovered by anyone who might still be lingering in the office after hours. He deepened his touch and she was powerless to prevent the low, earthy moan from escaping.

With her hand still on his cock, she braced her other hand behind her and wrapped her legs around his waist. Guiding him to her, she teased the head, first with the pad of her thumb, then by smoothing him over her feminine flesh slick with need. His dick flexed in her hand. Passion burned in his beautiful, dark brown eyes. He removed her hand. Her breath caught, then expelled on a soft moan when he joined their bodies.

Bracing her hands behind her, she used the desk to support her weight and she tightened her legs around him, then lifted her hips, riding the hot length of him. She set the pace, slow and easy until she needed more, more heat, more of him, then rode him faster and harder, taking every long, thick inch of him inside her until every muscle in her body strained in protest. She slowed, but he took over and quickened the tempo, holding her still and driving them closer to the edge of release.

The pressure inside her climbed, spiraling higher and higher until he sent her soaring. She flew apart and waves of intense pleasure slammed into her so hard she couldn't breathe. A cry tore from her lips and he cupped a hand behind her head and kissed her, swallowing her whimpers of pure ecstasy.

She clung to him, struggling for breath, willing her heart rate to slow, and in that one instant before he found his own release, she realized with a sudden burst of clarity the question of their future had never fully been hers to answer. Her heart had already made that decision seven years before—the night they'd eloped.

He cupped her face in his hands and kissed her. Sweet tender, and so full of emotion her heart gave a sudden lurch. The question wasn't whether or not they loved each other—in that respect, she had no doubts— but rather if he could love her once he knew the truth about her.

He ended the kiss and lifted his head. The deep affection in his gaze gave her hope and terrified her all at the same time.

"Come home with me."

"Tonight?" She couldn't. She wasn't ready. Not until she told him everything. In Napa he'd asked her to move in with him again, but the choice no longer belonged to her, but to him. For him to make an informed decision, he'd need all the facts.

But not yet.

She panicked at the thought of telling him. Once she told him the truth, that she'd lied to him to protect her secrets, and herself, the gentleness in his eyes would be extinguished for good. Regardless of how selfish, she wanted to savor the moment just a while longer.

"Tonight. Tomorrow night." He planted a quick, hard kiss on her lips. "Every night for the next fifty years."

She let out a sigh and slowly eased away from him.

As much as she'd like nothing more, she just couldn't go home with him. Not tonight. Not tomorrow. Not until she told him everything, and now was not the time or place to have that particular discussion.

She scooted off her desk, straightened her dress and searched for her panties. "That isn't a good idea," she said, plucking her thong from the arm of her chair.

She kept her back to him and stepped into her panties. By the time she turned back to face him, he'd finished tucking in his shirt and zipped up his trousers. Her heart plummeted at the thunderous expression on his face.

But she wasn't wired to placate wounded egos. When she sensed a threat, she went on the offensive. She hated herself for what she was doing, but she didn't know any other effective method of protecting herself.

"Don't start," she warned him.

"Don't start?" he repeated. She wasn't fooled. She knew him well enough to detect the tight control in his voice. The hard set of his jaw ranked as a fairly obvious indicator, too.

She picked up her shoes. One by one her emotions clicked off like a series of switches.

First anger.

Click.

She slipped into her shoes.

Caring next.

Click.

"You got what you came for," she said coolly. "Let's just enjoy the moment and call it a night."

"You think that's why I came to see you? For sex?"

Goodbye, pain.

Click.

She stuffed the Delaney file and two others into her briefcase. Not that she seriously believed she'd actually work on them, but she needed to keep moving or she'd end up turning those switches back on and falling apart again.

"Didn't you?" She shot him a chilling glance. "Get yourself a nice hard-on and know just who'll spread her legs for you, don't you?" she taunted, coating her voice in sarcasm. "The little woman."

The string of curse words he peppered her with put her potty-mouth to shame.

She folded her arms and tilted her hip to the side. "Are you about finished?"

Cold, hard fury flared in his eyes. "Yeah," he said with an equal chill. "I am."

The finality of his words hit her with the force of a hurricane, tearing the roof off her flimsy protective barrier. In her head, she heard a succession of clicks.

He stalked around the desk, scooped up his jacket from the guest chair, then pulled a business-size envelope from the pocket and tossed it on her desk.

"I'll see you in court," he said, then left without another word.

She covered her mouth with her hand and stared at the envelope, afraid to move. She couldn't open it. Later. She'd open it later.

Oh, God, what had she done?

Hello, heartache.

She'd ticked him off but good this time. Surely he wouldn't serve her with a petition for divorce. He wouldn't. She *knew* he wouldn't.

She prayed he hadn't.

Tucking the envelope into her briefcase, she gathered her things. She closed up her office, then let out a groan as she read the handmade sign someone had taped to her door: Honeymoon Suite—Do Not Disturb!

"I HATE MEN," Mikki complained to Lauren later that night. She adjusted the cordless phone and held it in place with her shoulder while she stirred the macaroni and cheese. "And they call *us* sensitive and emotional? We could take lesson from them."

"They can't help it," Lauren agreed sympathetically. "Maybe it's their DNA."

Mikki returned her pathetic excuse for dinner to the microwave to cook for another two minutes. "This never would've happened if he hadn't gotten his Jockeys in a knot," Mikki muttered, stalking to the fridge for a diet soda, wishing she hadn't left the bag from Felucca's on her desk.

"He should know you better."

"You would think." She slammed the fridge closed. "Argh!"

"So?" her sister prompted. "Are you going to open it?"

Mikki bit her lip and turned to stare at the envelope she'd laid on the kitchen table. Blank. White. Mocking. "Lauren, you don't think…"

"Divorce?"

She walked to the table, lifted the envelope and tested the weight in her hand. Six, maybe seven or eight sheets, she estimated. "Uh-huh."

Lauren sighed. "There's only one way to find out."

"Why couldn't I have just lied and said I was tired or had an early day in court tomorrow? That would have been easier, wouldn't it?"

"You don't know how to take the easy way out," Lauren chastised. "It's not in *your* DNA."

"And why is that?" Mikki didn't expect an answer. She'd called Lauren because she'd needed to rant and knew her sister would make all the right sympathetic noises and not badger her with tough questions she didn't want to answer.

"Is there something seriously wrong with me that I have be in a constant state of chaos?" She dropped into the ladder-backed chair. "I shouldn't have gotten so defensive." She closed her eyes. "Lauren," she whispered, "what if I pushed him too far this time?"

"Where's the envelope?" Lauren asked, her tone turning brisk.

"In my hand."

"Open it."

Mikki hesitated. "Lauren…"

"Do it quick," Lauren told her. "Like ripping off a bandage. If you do it fast, it won't hurt as bad."

"You know that never works," Mikki countered wryly, although she appreciated the sentiment.

Lauren chuckled.

"Okay, here goes." Mikki tore open the envelope. Her fingers trembled and she ended up ripping the envelope wide open just so she could remove the documents. Slowly she unfolded them and read the caption. "That bastard!"

"Oh, Mikki," Lauren said in a rush. "Honey, I'm sorry."

"No, it's okay," she said and laughed, feeling utterly and completely relieved. "It's not what we were thinking."

"Thank God." Lauren sounded just as relieved. "Well?" she prompted anxiously.

"Nolan's trying to stop the adoption of one my kids. It's only a request to the court to issue a temporary order granting his client supervised visitation privileges."

"So now what happens?" Lauren asked.

"I need to talk to a few people first, but I don't know that I'll oppose it."

"I was referring to Nolan."

"Oh." The microwave dinged. Mikki rose from the table feeling tons lighter. Her problems with Nolan were nowhere near solved, but she still hoped that maybe they could at least face the problems that had separated them in the first place. She had no idea if they could even reach a resolution, but she understood that hope was what she needed to cling to now. Without it, she had nothing left.

"After I tear him a new one for scaring me the way he did? It'll depend on him," Mikki said. "I thought this was all about me and my problems, but it's more than that." She related her conversation with Rory and how she'd put off talking to Nolan all week. "I realized tonight that what I'm really afraid of is that he might decide I'm not worth the trouble."

Lauren quietly asked, "Do you think maybe Nolan wanted to scare you so you'd make a decision?"

Mikki shrugged without thinking and tore the plastic film from the dish of mac and cheese. "I don't know. Maybe," she admitted.

"Did it work?"

The distinct note of humor lacing her sister's voice made Mikki laugh. "Like a charm."

13

"THE MICHAELSONS AREN'T pleased," Maureen said, her displeasure obvious in the sharpness of her tone. "If I'm being honest, I'm not too thrilled with you, either."

Mikki cranked the steering wheel to the right, turning the tires into the curb before killing the engine. She hated parking on an incline, and the one outside the house on Telegraph Hill was steeper than she was usually comfortable with. Her cell phone beeped a low battery signal.

"You read the psych eval," she reminded Maureen. "And so did the judge. She was going to grant the request anyway."

"Not if you had objected."

"I wouldn't have," Mikki said without an ounce of regret. "Keeping Zoe from establishing a relationship with her mother will cause her more harm than good."

"But the Michaelsons—"

"Aren't my problem and will just have to get over it," Mikki said firmly. "I don't care if I didn't score points with the Michaelsons, or you. My job is to look out for Zoe and what's best for her, and that's exactly what I did."

Mikki expected her decision to recommend supervised visitation wouldn't be a popular one, but Zoe was being given an opportunity that many in her situation were never afforded. Whether or not mother and daughter could even establish a bond remained to be seen, but for now, they were both being given a second chance.

"But that woman…"

"Isn't the same frightened girl that made a horrible mistake." Mikki pulled her keys from the ignition. "People change, Maureen. They grow up and deserve a shot at making things right." Which is exactly what she planned to do, provided Nolan was willing to give *her* a chance.

Maureen let out an exasperated sigh. "I hope you're right about this, Mikki."

She knew she was right. When it came her clients, she didn't take chances.

"What do I say to the Michaelsons?"

"Not to get their hopes up," Mikki cautioned.

"Give me the best case scenario."

"Zoe stays with John and Bobbie until the shrinks are all in agreement reuniting her with her mother won't exacerbate the separation anxiety and abandonment issues. Don't worry, Maureen," Mikki told her friend. "I'll make sure Zoe's okay."

Her cell phone beeped again. "My battery's dying. I'll call you next week, okay?"

"Real quick," Maureen said before she could disconnect. "How did this get before the judge so fast?"

Mikki's lips twitched. "Guess the Baylor name comes in handy."

"Figures Nolan would be behind this," Maureen complained sourly.

"Nolan's not the only Baylor in this town." Mikki's smile widened into a grin as Maureen made a few noises of disbelief. "Gotta run. Call you next week," she said, and disconnected the call.

Mikki slid her phone into the side pocket of her purse, set the parking brake and exited the car. Maureen's reaction had been mild in comparison to the absolute shock on Nolan's face when the judge informed him and the Michaelsons' attorney that *Mrs.* Baylor had requested the parties meet in an expedited ex parte in chambers to discuss an amicable resolution in the Delaney matter.

The decision to use her married name hadn't been premeditated, but was a last-minute snap judgment, made moments before she'd placed the call to the judge this morning. She'd known the reference would stun her husband clear down to his expensive wing tips, but she'd been a bargain shopper for too long not to know a great two-for-one deal when she saw one.

After her conversation with Lauren last night, Mikki had called Nolan several times. Either he hadn't gone home after leaving her, or he had Caller ID and had chosen to ignore her calls. She'd been close to driving over to his place to finally bring the whole mess out in the open so they could deal with it, but she'd wised up in time. If he was too angry to pick up the phone and talk to her, with the emotional bomb she was about to drop, keeping her distance until his temper cooled was smart.

With the baseball game for company, she'd spent the remainder of the evening working on the Delaney file. Despite all the horrors Zoe had suffered at the hands of a monster, Mikki realized Zoe was still lucky in that she had two families willing to fight for her. Taking Zoe from the Michaelsons and forcing her to live with people who were virtual strangers was not the solution, nor was preventing her from having the chance to reestablish a bond with her natural mother. Whether by design or accident, Nolan's request for supervised visitation had been the perfect alternative.

Mikki always did her homework, and when she'd arrived at the office this morning, she'd looked up Judge Catherine Garvey in the Martindale Hubble directory. She suspected it was no accident the Delaney matter was before a judge who belonged to the same alumni association as Robert Turner of Turner, Crawford and Lowe, and she hadn't even hesitated to capitalize on that connection by using her married name.

She approached the locked gate and punched in the security code. She had no idea if Nolan was even home, and she hadn't bothered to call in case he planned to dodge her calls again. Climbing the brick steps up to the massive hillside structure, her insides quaked with nerves. Her hands weren't much better, she noticed, reaching for the bell. Her only advantage was her determination to just get this the hell over with once and for all.

She pressed the bell. Varying degrees of disappointment and relief rippled through her when a stout middle-aged woman with salt-and-pepper hair and suspicious green eyes answered the door.

Oh, what the hell... "Hi," she said cheerily, then laid her best win-'em-over smile on the woman. "I'm Mikki Baylor. Nolan's wife."

TWO AND A HALF hours later, Mikki had paced the study, the Italian marbled corridor, the formal dining room, the casual dining room, the formal living room, two guest rooms, the billiard room, the kitchen, utility area—and that was only the first floor. The grandfather clock in the study tolled eight times. She flinched with each bell.

Where is he?

She called Tuck to see if he'd seen or heard from Nolan, but he hadn't been home and his cell phone was either off or he was out of range. Damned Caller ID, she thought. If Tuck and Nolan were together, a call from Nolan's place would be highly suspect.

Nolan's housekeeper had left less than an hour after Mikki's arrival. If Nolan didn't show up soon, she'd have to explore the upper floors.

Her gaze drifted across the room. Being in such close proximity to a full liquor cabinet in her state of mind was a bad combination waiting to happen.

She toed off her high-heeled black pumps. Drumming her fingers on the arm of the brown leather arm chair, she stared at the crystal decanters.

One drink. A short one. Just to take the edge off.

With her gaze still locked on the crystal decanters,

she stood and walked slowly toward the cabinet. She plucked a matching tumbler from the silver tray and wondered which of the decanters held bourbon.

"What the hell do you think you're doing?"

She jumped at the rough sound of Nolan's voice. Her heart slammed into her ribs and ricocheted around in her chest. "Tempting fate," she snapped because he'd scared the living daylights out of her. Snagging a bottle of spring water from the shelf, she filled the glass.

"And if I hadn't walked in just now?" he asked, striding toward her. "Would you be pouring water in that glass or something a little stronger?"

"Stronger." She downed half the water, then said, "Cut me a break, Nolan. I'm trying to keep it together here. Okay?"

Oh, she was not handling this well at all. She'd had way too much time on her hands waiting around for him to make an appearance. She was too worked up, too nervous and just damned scared.

He bent to open the mini fridge hidden behind a door in the rosewood cabinet. He produced a can of soda. "Strong enough for you?"

"It'll do."

He tossed ice into two glasses and poured. "Nice going on Delaney," he said casually. "Thanks."

"I didn't do it for your benefit. Or your client's," she added, taking the glass he offered.

He walked to the sofa and sat. She tried to read him, but he'd gone all stoic on her. Figured. Just when she needed to be able gauge his reaction, he clammed up tighter than George Steinbrenner during contract negotiations.

"Where have you been?" she asked.

A single dark eyebrow lifted. "Worried?"

She frowned. "As a matter of fact, yes." Worried that he'd hate the sight of her before the night was over.

"I was at the office," he said, loosening his tie. "Handing in my resignation."

"Your what?"

"I told Turner where he could shove his partnership," he said, raising his glass in mock salute before taking a long drink.

He gave her that silly, lopsided grin she adored. "Sorry, honey, but things are gonna be a little tight around here for a while. Your husband just quit his job."

She shot him an impatient glance. "Can you be serious for one minute, please?"

"I am serious. You know how much I hate franks and beans."

"What happened, Nolan?"

He rested the glass on his knee and dropped his head against the back of the sofa. "The firm's policy and ethics were in direct conflict with mine."

She frowned. "Meaning?"

Her breath caught at the cold dark fury in his eyes when he looked at her. "Meaning I won't have my wife's background investigated behind my back," he said, his voice rising. "What they turned up on you was privileged, and a violation of your rights. I should've walked the day Turner handed me that damned file."

"You had the partnership to—"

"Screw the partnership. And the partners." He released a long breath. "If you want to sue, you can be my first client."

So, she thought, sipping her soda. Nolan planned to start his own firm. She didn't doubt he'd be hugely successful, or that his decision to strike out on his own had been an immediate one. They hadn't discussed it, but then, communication outside of the bedroom wasn't exactly their forte.

"Mind if I ask what you're doing here?" he asked her, dragging her out of her thoughts. "I'm assuming you used the Mrs. Baylor card to get past the housekeeper, too."

"Noticed that one today, did you?"

"Hard to miss."

She thought she saw his lips twitch, but she wasn't going to hedge her bets quite yet. Those eyes were still a little too hard for her to be completely convinced he wasn't going to make her squirm.

"In the neighborhood and hoping to get laid?"

Ouch.

Definitely more squirming. No less than she deserved after the way she'd behaved last night. "I wouldn't rule out the possibility."

She could really use smile right about now. Something, anything, to give her waning confidence a boost. "We need to talk."

He closed his eyes. "I'm listening."

He wasn't about to make this easy on her, but she couldn't keep up the mouthy routine for much longer.

She crossed the room to the chair and sat. "There's something I need to say that I've been avoiding all week. Longer, actually. Like, about nine years."

"That bad, huh?"

She nodded, but he still had his eyes shut. "I'm not the person you think I am. Or rather, the kind of person…" She blew out a stream of breath. "This isn't working." Working? It wasn't going to fly, period. "Can I ask you a question?"

He let out a sigh of his own and straightened. He set his glass on the side table, then took hers from her hand and placed it next to his. "What is this all about?"

"I can't have children," she blurted.

There. She said it. She really said it. So why didn't she feel the weight lifting miraculously off her shoulders?

Concern shifted across the hard planes of his face, softening his expression. "What do you mean…*can't*?"

"I mean, I can't, as in it isn't going to happen. Ever."

He nodded slowly, as if considering her answer. "Can't or won't?" he asked. "If you're physically incapable, that's one thing, but if you won't consider it a remote possibility, that's another."

Under his penetrating stare, she shifted nervously.

"I'm guessing *won't*," he said carefully when she only fidgeted more. "You're obviously afraid to tell me why. Is that why you always try to push me away?"

She bit down hard on her lip.

"Am I close?"

She let out the breath she'd been holding. "Any closer and you'll step in it."

"Will you tell me why?"

She dragged her purse from the floor beside the chair and fumbled inside for the emergency pack of cigarettes. She knew he'd cross-examine her, and until now, she thought she'd been prepared to answer his questions.

He took the purse from her and tossed it beside him on the sofa. "Mikki?"

She fisted her hands and dug her nails into her palms. "I'm afraid."

"I figured that much," he said dryly. "But of what?"

Her heart started pounding all over again. Heavy, hard, until she thought it would explode under the pressure. "What I might do to a kid."

The first glimpse of a smile touched his lips. "Nobody's perfect, Mikki," he said patiently. "Parents make mistakes all the time. Mine sure did. I'll bet Emma would tell you that much straight-up. Hell, even Tuck's folks admit to making a few, and they're the closest to model parents as I've ever seen."

"Are you forgetting I'm an alcoholic? That alone is more than enough reason. I'm sober now, but what about tomorrow? Or next year? Or the next ten? Trust me on this one, because I know what I'm talking about. A drunk for a parent is a hell of a lot worse than one who isn't there at all."

"With what you have to deal with every day, I can see how you'd feel that way, but—"

"This isn't about my work." She laughed, the sound filled with such cold bitterness it frightened her. "I'm talking personal experience."

"What do you mean?"

"Marco Correlli. My father." At his confused expression, she dropped her bomb, then plowed forward without waiting for it to detonate. "My parents weren't dead when I married you, Nolan. I lied. One morning my mom took me to school and that was the last time I ever saw her. My guess is she'd finally had enough of my drunken father using her then beating the shit out of her before he finished zipping up his pants."

He stared at her, silently, intently. She wished he'd speak. Say anything so she wouldn't have to continue.

"She ran away," she admitted. "She escaped the physical and verbal abuse, and left me with an abusive, alcoholic, sorry excuse for a human being. I can still remember coming home from school that day and being more frightened about the dirty dishes she'd left in the sink than I was about being left alone. I had to clean it up before he got home, but I didn't know how. I tried, because I was petrified he'd do the same horrible things to me that he did to her when he came home drunk."

"Did he?"

Emotion choked her, cutting off her air supply. She struggled for breath. She'd come to far to stop now.

She blinked back the moisture blurring her vision. "Yes, Nolan," she whispered. "He did. The first time he molested me, I was only six years old."

A fierce light entered his gaze and she waited for the revulsion to come. He swore, sharp and succinct, the single word filled with venomous fury she somehow understood was not directed at her.

"I'm sorry I lied to you," she said quietly. "But you need to try to understand that abuse survivors are great at keeping secrets. Sometimes even from ourselves. It's a matter of survival that the one therapist I did see for a while called a defense mechanism."

She sucked in a deep, steadying breath before continuing. "I figured if you thought I was too young to really remember my parents, then you'd have no reason to question me about them. No questions, then no risk of my accidentally revealing too much."

"Why are you telling me all this now?" he demanded, his voice sharp, angry.

Consciously she knew his outburst wasn't directed at her, but was nothing more than a spillover from the harsh reality she'd forced them both to face. She tried to take strength from that small detail, but she felt as if she'd been sucked dry of every emotion but pain.

"Because I don't want to lie to you any longer," she said, praying he could forgive her. "You said people change. They grow up. Well, I can't do that unless I at least try to make this right."

A muscle in his jaw twitched. He looked ready to explode, but she had to finish now that she'd finally started. Rory had been right. She'd been carrying around a burden for far too long that wasn't even hers to shoulder. The first step in ridding herself of the past would never be successful if she couldn't even trust herself enough to face the truth of what she'd endured at the hands of the one person she should've been able to trust above all others—her father.

"I know nothing about my mother, and haven't seen her since she left. It'll be two and a half years next week that I buried my dad, but he'd been dead to me a lot longer. At least consciously. Subconsciously, I don't know if I'll ever be rid of the son of a bitch."

NOLAN NEEDED TO MOVE. Now, before he said or did the wrong thing. His chest ached with such fierce pain, breathing took effort.

He came off the sofa and stalked the room. Anger vibrated through him, shaking every part of him with the force of a 9.0 quake. Not at Mikki, but at himself, for taking the easy way out and never pushing hard enough past the barriers she'd kept erected so he could see the truth she'd locked inside for so many years.

He'd never known true hatred until that moment. If the bastard that had dared to hurt the sweet, innocent child she'd been wasn't already dead, he'd could easily have killed him himself.

"Nolan?"

The sound of her voice ripped through him, so small and tentative. Nothing at all like the woman who'd sass all nine of the Supreme Court justices if she were given the chance.

"Say something." He could hear her take in an unsteady breath. "Please."

"I don't what I'm supposed to say, Mikki." He turned to face her and wished he hadn't. Moisture shimmered in her big blue eyes and sliced him up inside. "What questions am I supposed to ask? I don't have a goddamned clue how to handle this and I'm scared of screwing it up."

She stared up at him with those watery eyes, needing him, and he didn't have an inkling of how to help her. He almost wished he could say something to piss her off so she'd rip into him. *That* he knew how to handle.

He dragged his hand through his hair. "I'm sorry, Mikki," he said, because it was easy. "I'm so sorry for what you had to go through."

"Oh, God, don't pity me, Nolan. Contempt is much easier to swallow than pity."

"Contempt?"

She laughed, the sound so brutally chilling she frightened him. "Oh, yes, contempt. Revulsion. Disgust. All common reactions when people learn about the things a father can do to his own daughter," she said fiercely. "More than you might think. We don't carry all this shame around with us because it's fun, you know."

He was beside her before she finished. Crouched in front of her, he took her face in his hands. "None of what happened was your fault. You were a little girl and not responsible. You do know that, don't you?"

She closed her eyes and nodded. "I eventually figured that out when I was older, but it isn't always that easy to remember." Her hands closed around his and she lowered them to her lap. "I'm sorry, Nolan."

"Stop apologizing," he told her. "You have nothing to be sorry about."

"Oh, yes," she said, "I do. Because I didn't have the courage to tell you all this years ago, I wasn't honest with you. If I had been, maybe it would've saved us both a lot of unnecessary pain."

And wasted years apart, he thought.

"You wanted to know what my trigger was," she said. "What sends me for a bottle of bourbon. Regret. I didn't have the guts to be completely honest with you, about my past, the drinking, but what I regret the most is that I hurt you when I said I didn't love you."

Her fingers flexed and tightened, her nails digging into the backs of his hands. Not for strength, he thought, because she possessed more than enough for both of them, even if she didn't yet realize it. But he knew, and for now that would have to be enough. With time, maybe he'd be able to help her see it for herself.

"I didn't have the courage to face my fear. I can't have children, Nolan, because if there is one drop of that in me…"

"No," he said. "It's not possible, Mikki."

"You don't know that, and neither do I. I've already got one mark against me, I'm not willing to take that chance, and I was too afraid of what you'd think if I told you why I feel the way I do about having kids. So every time you were close enough to see, I panicked and pushed you away."

She squeezed his hands harder. "It was never that I didn't love you. But that I'm so afraid I could be just like them." Her voice caught, momentarily halting her words. "I'd rather live my life alone than ever risk hurting an innocent child," she finished on a whisper, incapable of masking her pain.

She let go of his hands and covered her face. Her shoulders shook and she finally cried. He gently urged her out of the chair and pulled her into his arms. He held her tight, close to his heart.

He didn't know if it was possible for anyone to love someone more than he loved Mikki. Her courage, her strength, her tough exterior shielding the loving, caring woman inside, protecting herself from a hurt so deep and dark he couldn't begin to fully understand it. He didn't know if she would ever change the way she felt about having a family, and he realized it didn't make a difference. Sure, he'd love a big, loud, crazy family like Tuck's, but he also knew, with absolute certainty that if he had to choose between having a family and Mikki, he'd choose Mikki because he didn't want to spend another day without her. He loved her and always had. It was a fact of his life he'd accepted a long time ago. Maybe, once they worked through the issues of her past, her fears of being a parent could be overcome, but he wasn't willing to let her go regardless of the final outcome.

Once the flow of her tears ebbed and she quieted, he tucked his hand beneath her chin and tilted her head back. "Just because you didn't have a fairy-tale childhood," he said gently, "doesn't mean you aren't entitled to your own happily-ever-after."

The barest hint of a smile teased her mouth and her left eyebrow slowly hiked upward. "You sound like a really bad movie of the week."

He brushed his mouth lightly over hers. "Sappy, huh?"

Her smile broadened a fraction. "Pathetic."

"I don't have all the answers," he said, sobering. "But we'll find them."

"I don't do well in therapy. All that skull-digging bothers me." She narrowed her eyes. "A lot."

With her control issues, he didn't doubt it for a second, but at least he finally understood. He didn't need to hear every last detail of her abuse, but they needed to talk to through it, that much he did know. "You go to AA, right?"

She nodded. "Group settings are more my speed."

"Then we'll see if we can find a group setting."

She stiffened and started to pull away from him. Rising, she paced the length of the study, her movements clipped, agitated, as she struggled to find her comfort zone again. She stopped just as suddenly, turning to face him, blasting him with those blue eyes full of determination. "Don't expect me to make you any promises."

"Okay," he agreed, relieved to see a glimpse of the woman he loved with all his heart. "Don't you expect me to walk away from us. We have to deal with this, Mikki. It won't be easy, but we can handle it."

"Abuse is a lot different than alcoholism, you know," she said, narrowing her eyes again. "It could change how you feel about me."

"Don't count on it."

"I'll never become one of those spineless, agreeable

little wives, so don't you think for a minute you're going to wake up to one some morning."

"God, I hope not," he said, slowly narrowing the distance between them.

"It won't happen," she decreed confidently, but he saw the fear and uncertainly lurking in her eyes. "Got it?"

He slipped his arms around her, hoping to dispel her fears. "Got it."

"And just because I've decided it wouldn't kill me to take your name, don't get any bright ideas that you can tell me what to do."

He couldn't help himself. He grinned. "Wouldn't dream of trying."

"Make sure you don't," she quipped sassily. She wreathed her arms around his neck, the tentative smile curving her lips fading. "I'll always be who I am, Nolan. Some things never change, and that includes me."

"I love who you are," he told her, and nudged her closer, pulling all those wild curves tight against him. He dipped his head and kissed her, taking his time, savoring every nuance of her mouth hot and open beneath his.

She pulled away, ending the kiss long before he was ready to let her go. "Are you sure?" she asked, uncertainty drifting into her voice. "All this isn't too hard to handle? Because if you want out, consider this your last shot at freedom."

He let out a sigh and chuckled. "My last shot, huh?"

Boy, did she have a lot to learn. His freedom ended the day she'd insulted him in the law library. "I'll take that under advisement, counselor. Anything else?"

"Just be sure this is what you want."

"Mikki," he said, tugging her close again. "Loving you is the one thing I've always been sure about."

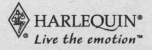

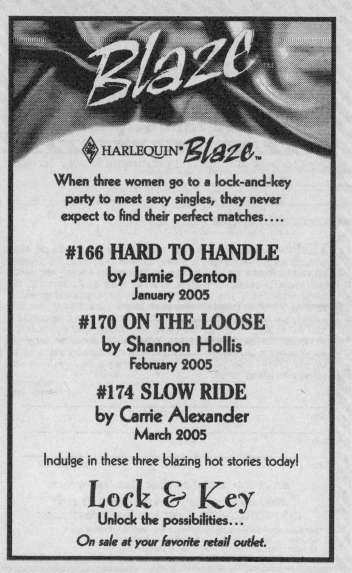

If you enjoyed what you just read,
then we've got an offer you can't resist!

Take 2 bestselling love stories FREE!

Plus get a FREE surprise gift!